Have Demon

John Brosnan was born ~~~~~~~~~~~~~~~~~~
for many years. He h~~~~~~~~~~~~~~~~~~~~
history of SF cinema, s~~~~~~~~~~~~~~~~~~
cinema. His novels include the *Sky Lords* trilogy and *The
Opoponax Invasion*. *Have Demon, Will Travel* is the sequel
to *Damned and Fancy*.

HAVE DEMON, WILL TRAVEL

John Brosnan

LEGEND

Published in the United Kingdom in 1996 by
Legend Books

1 3 5 7 9 10 8 6 4 2

First published in the United Kingdom in 1996 by
Legend Books

Random House UK
20 Vauxhall Bridge Road, London, SW1V 2SA

Random House Australia (Pty) Limited
20 Alfred Street, Milsons Point, Sydney,
New South Wales 2061, Australia

Random House New Zealand Limited
18 Poland Road, Glenfield
Auckland 10, New Zealand

Random House South Africa (Pty) Limited
PO Box 337, Bergvlei, South Africa

Random House UK Limited Reg. No. 954009

A CIP catalogue record for this book is
available from the British Library.

Papers used by Random House UK Limited are natural, recyclable
products made from wood grown in sustainable forests.
The manufacturing processes conform to the environmental
regulations of the country of origin.

Typeset by Deltatype Ltd, Ellesmere Port, Cheshire
Printed and bound in Great Britain by Cox & Wyman Ltd, Reading,
Berkshire

ISBN: 0 09 951231 9

Chapter One

'You think I'm insane, don't you?' Travis asked the police psychiatrist.

The psychiatrist, a benign-looking, balding man in his early forties, gave him a sad, disapproving little smile. 'I'm not comfortable with the word ''insane'', Travis. I would prefer to describe you as being in a very disturbed state.'

'Of course I'm feeling very disturbed,' said Travis heatedly, 'I've been bloody arrested!'

'Yes, but you must admit that your behaviour left the officers who'd been called to the scene no other option,' the psychiatrist quietly pointed out.

'I suppose so,' muttered Travis, 'And I'm sorry about what happened to that policewoman. But as I keep trying to tell everyone, it wasn't my fault. It was all down to those damn . . .' He stopped.

'Fairies?' said the psychiatrist. The police constable standing at the door of the interview room, sniggered.

'No, *demons*!' snapped Travis, 'I keep telling you that!'

'Ah, yes, demons. Sorry. And there are two of them?'

'Yes. Jack and Sharon. Except that Jack hasn't always been a demon. He used to be a Hollywood film producer. A tacky one. But Sharon's the real thing. She's a succubus.'

'Jack the demon who used to be a film producer,' said the psychiatrist slowly. 'And Sharon the succubus. Yessss. And, er, these two demons have been causing you problems, right?'

'Ever since we got back from Samella . . .'

'Ah yes . . .' The pyschiatrist glanced at his notepad then tapped his front teeth with his biro. 'Samella. This world you went to . . .'

1

'The world I was *sent* to!' corrected Travis. 'By Prenderghast!'

'And by Prenderghast you mean Gideon Leonard Prenderghast, the well-known computer games manufacturer. *That* Gideon Leonard Prenderghast?'

Travis sighed. He lit a menthol cigarette. He'd given up smoking years ago but recent events had driven him to resume the habit. 'He's not what he seems to be. He's not human! He's a . . . a *deity* of some kind. And not a nice one. He has incredible powers.'

'Travis, I've had a little chat with your editor at *Watchdog* magazine. He told me about your obsession with Mr Prenderghast. How you'd been working on your story – your planned exposé – for several weeks. Clearly you've become over-stressed by the pressure and now you're having these delusions as a result.'

Travis blew smoke at him, enjoying the disapproving wince on the pyschiatrist's face. 'I'm not having delusions. Look, doctor, do you want to hear my version of what happened or not?'

'Sorry. Please continue. And please call me Dave.'

Good grief, thought Travis. 'Okay, *Dave*, it was like this. When I confronted Prenderghast with what I'd found out about him he zapped me somehow and when I woke up I was on Samella, and in the company of Jack and Whiplash.'

'Whiplash?'

'He's the horse.'

'Oh, right,' said Dave, and scribbled some more in his notebook.

'Jack told me the score. I was going to be stuck on Samella until I found the Key, except that he didn't know what the Key was.'

'And this world, Samella, it was like Earth?'

'In some ways. I mean, there were people there and they spoke English. Or at least they did in the area where I ended up. But it was in a medieval era and there were things like dragons, fairies, elves, sorcerers and all that stuff.'

2

'And demons.'

'And demons,' agreed Travis.

'Tell me, Travis, were you a big fan of *The Lord of the Rings* when you were at school?' asked Dave.

'God, no! I never even got halfway through the first book.'

'But you read a lot of fantasy these days, right?'

Travis shook his head. 'No, I don't. I know the place sounds like a bad game of *Dungeons and Dragons* but that was nothing to do with me. That's the way it was! At first I thought it wasn't real. I was convinced that Prenderghast had hooked me up to some kind of incredibly sophisticated virtual reality device to teach me a lesson for meddling in his affairs. But eventually I had to admit to myself that Samella really did exist.'

'Of course,' said Dave, soothingly. 'And as you are now back here on Earth you obviously succeeded in finding this "Key" thing?'

'Yeah, with a lot of help from the Green Queen.'

'Who?'

'A goddess I ran into. The Queen of Mytherious Wood, the place where we had the final showdown with Prince Valerie, Sir Rodney, their two armies and that creep Damion.'

'I'm afraid you've lost me again,' Dave told him.

'Doesn't matter. Yes, I did find the Key . . .'

'And what was it?'

'It was a key.'

'The Key was a key?'

'Yes. The Key was a bloody key.'

'And what about the Door?'

'What Door?'

'The Door that the Key was for.'

Travis shook his head. 'There was no door, Dave. I simply wished on the Key and I was back home.'

'Very convenient for you.'

'Yeah, that's what I thought. And when I woke back in my own bed I thought for a while that it had all been a crazy

3

dream. But then I discovered I wasn't alone. In my kitchen I found Beatrice, Jack and Sharon.'

'Beatrice? She's another demon?'

'No, she's just a pain in the arse. She's also a princess.'

'What were they doing there?'

'Having breakfast and watching GMTV.'

'No, I mean why had they come back with you?'

'I haven't a clue! I was under the impression that once I found the Key my troubles would be over.' He stubbed out the cigarette. 'Instead they'd only just begun . . .'

As Travis stared in disbelief at Beatrice, Jack and Sharon the doorbell continued to ring.

'You've got a visitor, dickwit,' said Jack from his perch on top of the refrigerator.

'Oh God, it's probably Heather,' Travis groaned.

'She's your lover, isn't she?' asked Beatrice as she continued to nibble at a piece of toast.

'She was. I think my status is about to undergo a major review.' He ran his fingers through his hair. 'Sharon, quickly, disappear!'

'Why?'

'Because I don't want Heather to find a naked woman in my kitchen!'

'Why?'

'Just do it!'

'Oh, all right . . .' Sharon vanished.

Travis pointed. 'Jack, get in the fridge!'

'You're kidding. I'm not getting in the friggin' fridge. It's cold in there. I could freeze to death. And what if I run out of air?'

'Jack, you're no longer mortal. You're a demon. A bit of cold and a lack of oxygen isn't going to hurt you. And it won't be for long. Please!'

'Sheesh,' muttered Jack. But he fluttered down from the top of the fridge, opened the door and disappeared inside.

'What about me?' Beatrice asked him.

From the sound of the doorbell, Heather, if it was her – and he was pretty certain it was – was leaning on it. Heather, he knew only too well, had a bad temper. To Beatrice, 'Just stay where you are. With any luck I'll be able to get rid of her without her coming in here. But if she does, keep your mouth shut and let me do all the talking.'

'Sure,' she said, and started buttering another piece of toast.

Travis went out into the hallway and opened the front door. It was indeed Heather. She looked furious. Then her expression changed to one of surprise. She looked Travis up and down. 'Well, that's a great way to answer the door. What if it wasn't me?'

He remembered then he was just wearing his green y-fronts and his *Wasp Factory* tee-shirt. Then he remembered where his dressing-gown was. On Beatrice.

'And look at you!' continued Heather, now sounding puzzled. 'You look as if you haven't shaved for a week, and you *really* need a haircut. How did you get into this state in just two days?'

There was a good answer for that but Travis wasn't about to give it to Heather. Instead he muttered, 'It's hard to explain . . .'

Heather pushed by him. 'I imagine it's also hard to explain why you stood me up last night.' She headed for the kitchen. 'You didn't even bother to phone . . .'

He closed the door and hurried after her. 'I couldn't phone you, Heather. There weren't any phones where I ended up.'

'What about your mobile?' she asked as she entered the kitchen. Then she said, '*Oh!*'

Travis followed her into the kitchen. She had come to a dead stop and was staring at Beatrice who was sitting at the table in his dressing-gown. Beatrice was stunningly beautiful and even in his dowdy and frayed dressing-gown she looked every inch a fairy tale princess, which she was. Beatrice smiled at Heather and gave her a little regal wave with the piece of toast. 'Hello, Heather,' she said brightly.

5

Heather turned and looked at Travis. The icy stare from her blue eyes could have frozen a burning oil well. 'I'm all ears,' she said in a voice just as chilly.

Travis thought fast. Too fast, he would soon realize. 'Er, Heather, I'd like you to meet Beatrice. She's from, er . . . Australia.'

'Oh, really? And what's she doing here? And more importantly, what's she doing in your dressing-gown?'

'She's staying here for a while. And she forgot to pack her own dressing-gown so I loaned her mine.'

Heather gave him a look that made his balls quiver. His reaction was to dig himself into an even deeper hole. 'It's not what it seems. Beatrice is my . . . cousin.'

'You never told me you had relatives in Australia,' said Heather.

'Didn't I? Gosh. How strange. My uncle Robert, on my mother's side, immigrated out there years ago.'

Heather turned back to Beatrice. 'You're from Australia?'

Beatrice, though looking blank, nodded eagerly. 'Yes. I am.'

'You don't sound Australian. In fact, I can't place your accent at all.'

'It's Tasmanian,' said Travis quickly. 'Entirely different accent from the rest of Australia. Tasmania's an island, you know. Off the south coast . . .'

'I know where Tasmania is,' Heather said coldly, 'but I wasn't aware Tasmanians had different accents.'

'Well, they do,' Travis told her. 'Right, Beatrice?'

'Oh yes, we Tasminions have entirely different accents.'

'See?' said Travis. 'She even pronounces Tasmania differently.'

'Very well,' Heather said. 'So whereabouts in Tasmania do you come from, Beatrice?'

Beatrice looked helplessly at Travis. Just then there came a sneeze from inside the refrigerator. They all looked at the refrigerator. Then Heather said, 'What was that?'

'What was what?'

6

'It sounded like someone sneezed inside your fridge.'

'Nah. Must have been some ice melting,' said Travis. 'I'm, er, defrosting it.'

There was another sneeze, followed by an angry mutter.

Heather said slowly, as she stared apprehensively at the refrigerator, 'There's someone in your fridge, Travis.'

'Don't be ridiculous,' he laughed. 'How could anyone fit in there?' He wondered what her reaction would be if she opened the door and saw Jack.

The phone rang. *Thank God*, thought Travis as he snatched it up. 'Hello?'

'Travis, what the hell are you playing at?' demanded an angry voice. Travis groaned inwardly. It was his editor, Martin Shulman. 'You were going to call me immediately after your interview with Prenderghast and put me in the picture. I rang this number *and* your mobile for hours last night and got zilch. What happened?'

'Er . . . something unexpected came up. Sorry. Circumstances beyond my control and all that . . .'

'So what was the outcome with Prenderghast?' Shulman asked him eagerly. 'Did he confess?'

'Well, not exactly,' Travis told him.

'What's that supposed to mean?'

'There were complications,' said Travis. He glanced at Heather. She was still staring warily at the fridge but she hadn't made a move towards it. At least the mystery of the fridge had distracted her from the mystery of Beatrice. For the time being.

'Complications? But we can still run the story, can't we? I need it by the end of the day so the libel lawyers can give it the once-over.'

'I may have to postpone it, Martin. I'll have to try and talk to Prenderghast again.'

'*What*?' exploded Shulman. 'But you promised you'd have it all tied up by today. You know it's going to be the main feature in the next issue!'

'Martin, I'll call you back later and explain everything,'

Travis told him. 'But right now I'm kind of tied up. Bye.' He hung up on his editor before he could say anything else. He saw that Heather was now subjecting him to the same intense scrutiny that she'd given the fridge.

'Don't tell me your Prenderghast exposé blew up? After all your work?' she asked him.

'Something like that,' he admitted. 'As I told Martin, there are complications.'

'And you're not going to tell me what they are either, are you?'

'I will, but not right now. Later, I promise, when I've got a few things sorted out.'

She glanced again at Beatrice who smiled prettily back at her. 'Such as your Australian *cousin* here?' she said pointedly.

'Yes,' he admitted.

Heather nodded, clearly having made up her mind. 'I'm off to work. Call me later. When you can tell me all about your *complications*.' Then, after giving the refrigerator one more suspicious look, she marched out of the kitchen. Travis hurried after her. He caught up with her as she was going out the front door.

'There really is a good explanation for all this,' he told her, somewhat desperately.

She smiled and said, 'There'd better be.' Then she added, 'She's very pretty, your *cousin*.' And slammed the door shut behind her.

Travis sighed and returned to the kitchen. Sharon had reappeared and was having another cup of coffee. Jack was hammering on the inside of the fridge door and yelling, 'Lemme out of here, you bastards!' Travis opened the door and Jack tumbled out, shivering. He spread his wings and flew back to the top of the fridge. 'That was a great idea, dickwit. Next time *you* hide in the frigging icebox and I'll sort out your babe.'

'Sorry about that,' Travis told him, 'But it was all I could

8

think of on the spur of the moment. Pity you had to start sneezing.'

'You're lucky I didn't start farting. You'd have to throw all your food away. But I did learn something interesting from the experience.'

'You did? What?'

'The little light *does* go off when you close the door.'

The phone started ringing again.

'Travis, what is Australia?' Beatrice asked him.

'Hang on,' he said, as he reached for the phone. He feared it was Martin again. It wasn't. Travis was taken completely by surprise. He held out the receiver to Jack. 'It's for you.'

'Ah, that'll be Arnie,' Jack said, and took the phone.

'How the hell could anyone know you were here . . .?' asked Travis in amazement, but Jack was already talking to whoever this Arnie was. Travis wondered dazedly if it was Arnold Schwarzenegger.

The doorbell rang again. Had Heather returned? He doubted it.

'Beatrice, can I have my dressing-gown back please? Just for a moment?'

'No, you may not. I'm not wearing anything under it.'

'Please, don't tell me things like that while I'm having a panic attack.' He hurried into the bathroom. His tatty bathrobe was hanging behind the door. He put it on and hurried back to open the front door. It wasn't Heather, it was his picky downstairs neighbour, Mrs Whitby, a retired tax inspector. She gave him a disapproving look, as was her habit. 'Mr Thomson,' she said.

'Mrs Whitby,' he replied. Now that they had established their identities, Travis waited for her to state the reason of her visit. He knew it would be a complaint of some kind.

'Mr Thomson, there's an animal in my back garden and I have a strong suspicion that you are somehow involved with its presence.'

'Mrs Whitby, you know I don't have any pets. It's not

9

allowed here. It's probably the dog that belongs to that family across the road.'

'It's not a dog.'

'No? A cat then?'

'It's a horse, Mr Thomson. And it's eating my hydrangeas.'

Travis groaned. *Whiplash*.

Chapter Two

'Do you mind not smoking?' Travis asked Jack.

'Yeah, I do mind, dickwit,' said Jack and blew one of his special trademark series of three linked smoke rings. 'When you're a demon smoking comes with the territory.'

Travis was about to argue with Jack but surrendered to a wave of resignation. Instead he said, 'If you can't beat 'em, join 'em, I suppose. Can I have one?'

'Didn't know you smoked,' said Jack.

'I gave up years ago. But now I think I might start up again. For the duration.'

Jack shrugged and tossed him a Marlboro. Travis caught it and lit it on the gas ring. He inhaled and immediately felt light-headed. Or rather, even *more* light-headed than he had felt previously.

'Those things racing about down there – what are they called?' asked Beatrice. She was leaning out of the kitchen window. Travis had found her some of Heather's clothes and she was now dressed in a pair of jeans, a tee-shirt and one of his jackets. The jeans were a little too tight for her but he wasn't complaining. He joined her at the window and she pointed at the traffic in the street below.

'Those are . . . er, horseless carriages,' he told her.

'I can see *that*, silly,' she said, impatiently, 'but what exactly are they?'

'They're called motor cars,' he said tersely. 'And be very careful of them. Treat them as dangerous, unpredictable and clumsy animals with very, *very* small brains and you just might stand a fair chance of survival.'

One of Heather's skirts, topped by one of Travis's shirts, floated into the kitchen. The shirt detached itself from the above the skirt and flew across the room. It landed on the floor

11

at Travis's feet. Sharon materialised within the skirt which she immediately discarded, leaving her in all her usual, olive-skinned, magnificent nakedness. She stamped her foot. 'I won't wear clothes!' she declared.

'Good for you, babe,' approved Jack as he leered at her.

Travis sighed. 'Sharon, either you wear something or you'll just have to stay invisible the whole time you're here.'

'Fine with me,' said Sharon, and vanished.

'Spoilsport,' said Jack to Travis.

'I don't mean while you're in my flat,' Travis said, addressing empty air. 'Though admittedly I do find it a bit disconcerting . . .' *Hah!* 'But I thought you wanted to go out with us. It'll be more convenient for all concerned, and safer for you, if you remained visible when we go outdoors.'

Sharon reappeared. 'Do I have to? They make me feel all constricted. And they itch.'

'Just while you're here,' urged Travis. 'And it won't be for long. As soon as I can get in touch with Prenderghast and sort all this out you'll be back in your own world. Maybe before this very day is over.'

'I don't want to go back,' protested Beatrice. 'Not yet, anyway. I've hardly seen anything of this world yet.'

'I promised we'll do some sight-seeing before we go to Prenderghast's office,' Travis told her.

Personally, he was having doubts that it was all going to be as easy as he hoped. He'd tried ringing Prenderghast and had been told by his secretary that he was at a meeting. That, as he knew from experience, could mean anything. But surely Prenderghast would keep to his word – he'd found the Key, so that should be an end to it. Surely the fact that Jack, Beatrice and Sharon – and Whiplash – had accompanied him back here was some kind of cosmic bureaucratic error? Or had it been more, deliberately perverse mischief on Prenderghast's behalf? No, that didn't bear thinking about. He wouldn't be able to cope with this situation for very long without his entire life falling apart under the strain. For one thing it was going to cost him a lot of money – he had already spent a small fortune in getting the owners of a riding school in Primrose Hill to agree to come and collect Whiplash and house him in their stable for the time being. Beatrice kept demanding that he buy her some 'proper' clothes . . . and the food bill alone was going to be bloody enormous.

Then there was the small but perfectly formed problem of what he was going to tell Martin about Prenderghast: *'I was right, Martin, Prenderghast's virtual reality helmets for children do present a safety threat, but an even bigger one than I realized. I've found out that Prenderghast isn't just a crook but some kind of ancient dark god, and I suspect that those helmets are designed to suck out the children's life force to provide him with food . . . It's clearly a job for the Advertising Standards Authority.'*

And even in the unlikely event that Martin swallowed any of this without having Travis fitted for a designer strait-jacket, what would Prenderghast's reaction be when he found out that Travis was trying to spread the truth about him? He would probably send him somewhere even worse than Samella. And just when he was getting used to indoor plumbing facilities again.

'I want to meet your King and Queen,' announced Beatrice.

'You what?' asked Travis, distracted.

'I want to meet your King and Queen,' repeated Beatrice. 'You do *have* a King and Queen here don't you?'

'We have a Queen but no King. Not yet, at least. But we have loads of Princess and Princesses, Dukes and Duchesses, Viscounts and whatever. In fact, our extended Royal Family is so large it could provide the population of a small country. A lot of people here think that's exactly what it should do.'

'You mean there's a danger here of the commoners rising up in rebellion against your Royalty? she asked, sounding shocked.

'Hardly. Our commoners are a very apathetic bunch. Besides, if we didn't have a Royal Family there would be nothing to fill the tabloid newspapers with.'

13

'The what?' she said, blankly.

'The tabloid newspapers. They're papers for people who don't like reading.'

She frowned, then said, 'Very well, take me to meet your Queen then. Today.'

'Sure. Right. I'll ring her later and make an appointment for you.'

The phone rang again. And again it was the mysterious Arnie for Jack. As Jack took the call, Sharon, once again wearing the shirt and skirt, and fully visible, returned. 'Okay, I'll wear these but I draw the line at shoes. And underwear. I won't wear underwear.'

'Fine, fine,' he sighed.

'So how do I look?' He examined her. Even dressed she looked naked. But it was better than nothing. 'You'll pass for human,' he assured her. *Just*.

'Thanks, Arnie,' Jack told the phone, 'I'll get back to you.' He hung up and muttered, 'The bitch!'

'Arnie's a bitch?' asked Travis.

'No, my wife Candice is the bitch. She's screwing me behind my back.'

'Sounds exactly like your cup of tea,' laughed Travis.

But Jack just scowled. 'Arnie told me that since I disappeared she's had me declared dead and taken over my film company. She's fired my staff, hired her own faggy people and changed the name from Pulp Productions to New Age Life Productions. She's churning out videos on meditation, channeling and aromatherapy! Shit!'

'Is she making money?'

'Yeah, dammit. That *really* gets up my nose.'

'So what are you going to do?'

'I don't know yet. I told Arnie I'd call him back when I'd thought of something.'

'So when are we going to call your Queen and set up an appointment for me?' interrupted Beatrice.

'Later,' Travis assured her. He turned back to Jack. 'Just who is this Arnie?'

'An old pal of mine. We started in the business at the same time. Worked for Corman like me. Now he's a publicity agent.'

'And he's in Hollywood, right?' asked Travis slowly.

'Sure.'

'You've been calling Los Angeles on *my* phone?' Travis tried to remember how much it cost a minute to call the USA.

'Hey, keep your shirt on. I'll pay you back.'

'How?' Travis asked him. 'This may come as a shock to you, but I doubt if you'll find anything suitable in the Situations Vacant columns for a smelly, demon midget who, apart from being able to fly and spit fire, doesn't seem to possess any noticeable commercial talents.'

'Yeah?' Well, for your information, smart-ass, I may just surprise you on that front.'

'Surprise me,' demanded Travis, sceptically.

'Not yet. I'm still working on the angles . . .'

'What angles?'

Jack tapped the side of his nose and winked at Travis. 'Trust me. I know what I'm doing.'

'That's a scary thought. Just how do you plan to . . .' He stopped. The doorbell was ringing again. 'Oh no . . . now what?'

'You always this popular?' Jack asked.

'Not usually. Quick, hide again!'

'I'm not getting back in the icebox. No way.'

'Hide in the bathroom then! And be quiet this time!'

Jack fluttered out of the kitchen. Travis looked at Beatrice and Sharon. 'Try and act . . . normal,' he told them, helplessly.

With mounting trepidation he went into the hallway and opened the door. Waiting outside was Stephen Hastings. Stephen was his closest friend. They had met at university. Stephen was a journalist too, but a freelance one specializing in science reporting. The same age as Travis – thirty – he was a tall, athletic-looking man with thinning red hair. He wore thick glasses that emphasized his blue eyes. Normally Travis was always pleased to see Stephen but this particular morning was an exception. 'Oh, it's you,' he said, without enthusiasm.

Stephen grinned his usual cheery grin. 'Don't go overboard with excitement, Travis.'

'What are you doing here?'

'Heather called me from work. Sounded a mite upset. Gave me a weird story about you and a gorgeous Australian cousin. Naturally I was intrigued . . .' He attempted to enter but Travis stuck out his arm.

'It's really not convenient right now, Stephen. I'm up to my eyes in . . . well, *everything*.'

'Now I'm even more intrigued. And I know for a fact that you don't have any relatives in Australia. And from the sound of it, Heather knows it too. So what's going on. Who is she?'

'I promise I'll tell you everything later, when I've got a breathing space.'

Stephen's grin grew wider. 'That sounds fun. She exhausting work, your *cousin?*' He easily brushed by Travis and entered the hallway.

'Bugger,' muttered Travis, and followed after Stephen. Stephen came to a sudden stop in the kitchen doorway, causing Travis to bump into him.

'*Two* gorgeous women!' said Stephen in surprise. 'Heather only mentioned one.'

Beatrice, leaning with her back to the window, and Sharon, sitting at the table, smiled at Stephen. Travis saw something in the way that Sharon was regarding Stephen that worried him. And to his eyes the sexual aura that always surrounded Sharon seemed to have been increased in voltage. Bad news.

'So please introduce me to these two charming ladies,' Stephen told him.

'Ah, that's Beatrice . . . and that's Sharon . . .' He pointed them both out. 'And Beatrice, Sharon . . . this is Stephen, an old friend of mine.'

They all exchanged helloes. Then Stephen said, 'And which of you is Travis's cousin from Australia?'

'I am,' said Sharon.

16

'No, *I* am,' said Beatrice, frowning at Sharon. 'Travis *said* I was. Didn't you, Travis?'

'Uhhhh,' said Travis.

Stephen, obviously enjoying himself, grinned at Travis. 'So? Which one is your cousin?'

'Uhhhh,' said Travis, 'they both are.'

'You have *two* Australian cousins now,' laughed Stephen. 'This is getting better and better.'

'Yes, well . . . it's true,' said Travis, painfully aware of how lame it all sounded.

'And are you sisters as well?' Stephen asked Beatrice and Sharon.

'No! Of course not!' said Beatrice, offended. 'I'm a human being with royal blood. Sharon's just a succubus.' Then Beatrice said to Sharon, 'No offence, Sharon.'

Sharon reacted with a haughty sniff.

Stephen looked at Travis then back at Beatrice. 'You've lost me there. Royal blood? Succubus?'

'Ooops,' said Beatrice. 'Sorry, Travis.'

Stephen looked enquiringly at Travis again, his grin replaced by a suspicious frown. 'What's going on? Is this all some sort of leg-pull? Have I been set up?'

'Set up?' said Travis. 'No, no. Beatrice is just a little confused. Suffering from jet lag. And exhaustion. It was a long flight.'

'You're still sticking to the Australian scenario?' asked Stephen. 'Come on, Travis, come clean. What's the real story? Who are they? And what are they doing here?'

Travis decided, desperately, to try a different approach. 'I can't tell you that. It's confidential. All I can say is that it's to do with my work. The Prenderghast assignment I told you about.'

'Your big story on him? You've cracked it?'

'Yes. And it's even bigger than I thought. And dangerous. That's why Beatrice and Sharon are staying here . . . for the time being. They're involved in the whole situation. They've

17

provided me with vital information and as a result . . .' Travis made a dramatic pause.

Stephen suddenly became all serious. 'You mean Prenderghast might do something . . . rash? Because of what you've found out about him?'

'Exactly.'

Stephen looked at the two women. 'And you two are hiding out here? From Prenderghast?'

They exchanged a glance then both solemnly nodded.

'Wow,' said Stephen. He turned to Travis. 'I know you've been telling me that the Prenderghast thing was going to be big, but I had no idea . . .'

'Neither did I,' said Travis. 'So you'll understand if I don't tell you any more until it's all out in the open. Safer that way for all concerned. Understand?'

'Sure, sure. I understand,' Stephen assured him.

'I like you,' Sharon suddenly announced to Stephen.

Taken by surprise, Stephen just gaped at her for a few moments, then went into preening mode. Travis saw him visibly swell up. 'You do?' said Stephen to Sharon. 'Well, I'm flattered. And I like you too. And I'd certainly like to know you better.'

Travis stifled a groan. Sharon was giving off so much sexual magnetism he was surprised that every single piece of cutlery in the kitchen wasn't launching itself in her direction. The last thing he needed was Sharon getting her deadly teeth into Stephen.

'When all this Prenderghast business is finished with you must let me take you to dinner,' Stephen told Sharon.

'I'd like that. Very much,' she simmered.

Travis gripped Stephen firmly by an elbow and began to steer him towards the door. 'I think it's time you were leaving. The girls and I have a lot to do.' He managed, despite Stephen's protests, to manoeuvre him out into the hallway. 'I'll call you, Sharon!' Stephen cried.

'Please do!' came Sharon's reply. 'I can't wait!'

'Stephen, stay away from her!' Travis whispered fiercely. 'You have no idea what you're dealing with!'

'Oh, I think I have a pretty good idea.'

'No, seriously! She can be . . . kind of lethal!'

'Sounds better and better.'

'I mean it. Stay away from her. Anyway, she won't be around here for much longer. I hope.'

'So whereabouts does she live usually?'

'A long way away. Put her completely out of your mind. Pretend she doesn't exist.' He kept trying to push Stephen towards the front door but Stephen was resisting.

'What's got into you, *friend*? A drop-dead gorgeous woman makes a pass at me and you're doing your damnedest to keep us apart!'

'Believe me, it's for your own good. And you're spot on with the "drop-dead" part.'

'Oh, *sure*. Look, since Carol walked out on me two months ago I've been practically celibate. Almost. And that Sharon is out of this world.'

It was very tempting but Travis bit his tongue. He pushed Stephen again.

Stephen muttered, 'I'd be crazy not take up an invitation like that from someone like her.'

'And you'd be crazier still if you did. Now please get out of here. I'll explain everything as soon as I can.' He opened the door.

Stephen reluctantly exited. 'I'm not giving up, Travis. Tell Sharon I'll be in touch.'

'Bye Stephen,' said Travis and slammed the door on him. He marched back into the kitchen. 'Well done, girls. I ask you to act normal and you drop me in it again.'

'I was acting normal,' said Sharon, huffily.

Jack flew into the kitchen and landed on the TV set. 'Who was that dork?'

'My best friend,' Travis told him.

'That figures,' said Jack.

'I thought he was cute,' said Sharon, raising her arms and giving a sinuous stretch.

'I could see that. Promise me you'll leave him alone. I don't want my best friend ending up as a metaphysical snack-on-a-stick for you.'

'I won't even take the smallest bite of his soul. It's his body I'm interested in.'

'Well, don't take any bites out of that either,' said Travis, remembering what she'd done to the boy sorcerer, Damion.

'Travis?' said Beatrice.

'Yes, what is it?' he asked her impatiently.

'Can we go and see your Queen now?'

Chapter Three

Prince Valerie sat slumped in his throne, chin cradled in the palm of his hand. He was not a happy bunny. He didn't even bother to acknowledge the presence of the page who was nervously clearing his throat as he approached him.

'Your Highness . . . ?' said the page tentatively.

'What is it?' asked the Prince without interest.

'Your sorcerer, Damion, has returned, sire. He wishes an audience with you.'

The Prince looked up in surprise. 'Damion? Here?' And, yes, it was true. There was Damion standing in the doorway – haggard, bowed and looking much older than his true years, but unmistakeably Damion. 'Damion! You're alive!'

Supported by a walking stick, Damion, clad in his usual black, shuffled into the throne room. 'More or less, my Lord, as you can see.'

'Fetch him a chair at once!' the Prince ordered the page. The page scuttled away and returned almost immediately with a chair. He placed it beside Damion and helped the weakened sorcerer sit down on it.

'It's good to see you, Damion,' the Prince told him. 'I'd presumed you'd fallen victim to the Green Queen, like everyone else.'

'No, she let me go . . .' He made a face. 'But not without my paying a price.'

The Prince decided it would be prudent of him not to enquire about the nature of the price involved. 'And where have you been all this time?'

'I spent some weeks recuperating at S.C.O.S.'

'S.C.O.S.?'

'The Sanitarium for Clapped-Out Sorcerers. But what of you, my Lord? How did you escape on that terrible day?'

The Prince waved a dismissive hand. 'Oh, I managed to turn myself into a night screet just in the nick of time. I was able to fly out of Mytherious Wood before I succumbed completely to the Green Queen's magic. I flew back here and have been trying to sort out the shambles ever since. Haven't made much progress. There are a lot of disgruntled people around. I mean, losing an entire army doesn't inspire much confidence in a ruler.'

'Actually, my Lord, it was *two* armies . . . if you include King Morbia's.'

The Prince grimaced. 'Don't remind me. King Morbia keeps sending me invoices, not only for his missing men but for all the horses, weaponry and equipment. My accountants are tearing their hair out. Plus my social life has gone to hell in a bucket.'

'Because of your missing army?'

'Partly, but mainly because I was outed as a vampire by you-know-who.'

'Oh, of course. I forgot.'

'I wish everyone else would. Dinner party invitations are a thing of past, the locals keep giving me a wide berth and I have to travel miles to get a decent drink.'

'You have my deepest sympathy, my Lord,' said Damion. 'And you might be interested to know that when I had recovered some of my strength I attempted to pick up the trail of you-know-who and our other mutual friends.'

The Prince leaned forward eagerly. 'Were you successful?' he asked.

'At first. My treacherous succubus left enough of a spoor for me to follow. I followed it as far as Lankhair. And there it ended.'

'Why?' asked the Prince, disappointed.

'It ended at the premises of a certain Jeremy P. Best. Perhaps you've heard of him.'

The Prince frowned. 'Rings a bell, but please refresh my memory.'

'He's the quest fixer. ''Why Waste Time on Quest When You Can Go to Best'' is one of his advertising slogans.'

'Oh, yes. I do know of him.'

'He told me – for a fee – what happened. Unluckily he had already acquired the object that you-know-who was seeking. The object known as the Key.'

'Shit,' muttered the Prince. 'So you-know-who was able to return to his own world?'

'I'm afraid so, my Lord. The odd thing was that his three Sammelian companions went with him. And his horse too.'

'Did they?' asked the Prince, surprised and annoyed. 'That means they've all moved beyond our reach.'

'Not all. Best told me that you-know-who was accompanied by only three others. From his description they were Princess Beatrice, my Sharon and Jack, the flying fart merchant. Annabelle was not present. My guess is that she remained in the domain of the Green Queen.'

'Then she is just as safe from us,' sighed the Prince. 'I dare not ever challenge the power of the Green Queen again.'

'Ah, but perhaps she is the safest of them all. Perhaps the others are not beyond our reach . . .' Damion gave what now passed for a smile on his ravaged features.

'What are you saying?' demanded the Prince.

'I'm saying that I believe it's possible that we can follow you-know-who and the others to his world. You and I, my Lord. Though I must warn you that there will be serious risks involved.'

The Prince thought for a time, then he said, 'I thirst for revenge even more than I thirst for blood. Damn the risks, let's *do* it!'

For the first time in quite a long while, Damion laughed.

'I'm afraid Mr Prenderghast isn't here, Mr Thomson,' the secretary coolly informed Travis. 'He had to leave the country on urgent business.'

'He's gone abroad?' cried Travis. 'The last time I rang he was in a meeting!'

'As I said, it was all very unexpected.'

'Where is he then? Haven't you a number where I can reach him?'

'I'm not allowed to pass on such information,' she told him.

'Can you tell me when he'll be back?'

'I'm afraid not. He didn't say.'

'Good grief . . .' sighed Travis.

'But he did ask me to give you a message, Mr Thomson.'

'He *did*?' asked Travis, his hopes rising. 'Well, what is it?!'

'He told me to tell you he would be thinking about you.'

His hopes crash-landed. 'Is that it? That's the entire message?'

'Yes. That's it, Mr Thomson. Glad to have been of assistance. Goodbye.' She hung up.

Travis stared impotently at the handset before slamming it down.

'Temper, temper,' chided Jack.

'Prenderghast has left the country. For an indefinite period it seems. But he left me a message – he will be thinking about me.'

'Oooo. I'm not sure I like the sound of that,' said Jack.

'Neither do I. He's toying with me.' Travis slumped into an armchair. 'What the hell do I do now?'

'You take me to meet your Queen,' said Beatrice brightly.

Travis looked at her. 'This going to come as a bit of a shock, but I am not on speaking terms with the Queen of England.'

Beatrice frowned. 'You mean you've had an argument?'

'No, you royal prat, I mean I've never met her. We move in different social circles. Which therefore means I can't give her a call and tell her I'm dropping round for afternoon tea with a friend. Got it?'

Beatrice looked both disappointed and annoyed. 'Well, that wasn't very nice – leading me on that way. Don't you know any royalty at all?'

24

'Only you. Unfortunately.'

Now she looked hurt and Travis immediately felt guilty. 'Hey, I'm sorry. I didn't mean that.'

'Yes, you did,' she said, lower lip aquiver. 'And after all the times I saved your life.'

'You *what*? It was *me* who saved *your* life on occasions too numerous to count. I saved you from that bloody dragon, I saved you from Bovrol the Barbarian, from Prince Valerie . . . from *everything*.'

'Not as many times as I saved your life,' she said firmly. 'If it wasn't for me you would have been torn apart by that mob of angry barbarians after that duel . . . and I persuaded Prince Valerie to give you a weapon when Sir Rodney was going to run you through where you stood . . .'

'Hah! Don't talk to me about your dear Prince Valerie – if it wasn't for me you'd be spending your days sleeping next to him in a coffin and spending a fortune on dental floss!'

'Ahem,' said Jack. 'What about me? Who got you all out of Prince Valerie's castle? And who flew you away from Sir Rodney's men?'

'All of which would have been impossible without *my* help,' added Sharon.

'Oh, what's the use,' muttered Travis. 'Okay, we've all saved each other's lives. Let's leave it at that and hope we won't be put in any more life-threatening situations.' He looked at Beatrice. 'I can't take you to Buckingham Palace but to make up for it I'll take you to Harrods instead.'

'What's "Harrods"?' she asked.

'A different kind of palace. You'll love it. We'll go as soon as I've changed my clothes.' He was about to head for the bedroom when Jack suddenly asked if he had a polaroid camera. 'Yes, I do,' he told Jack. 'Why?'

'I want to borrow it, that's why.'

Travis went and fetched his polaroid camera from his bedroom and gave it to Jack. When he returned to his bedroom and opened his wardrobe he got a surprise. Hanging in there were the clothes he'd last been wearing in Samella,

25

courtesy of Prince Valerie. And sitting on the floor of the wardrobe – and looking just as out of place as the garish Samellian outfit – was the Colt .45.

He gingerly picked it up and examined it, wondering if it would still work in this world. He was tempted to pull the trigger but told himself that even by his recent standards of behaviour that would be an extremely silly thing to do. He put it on the shelf and covered it with a towel. Even if it did work he wouldn't be needing it in London.

When he'd changed his clothes and went back into the kitchen he found Jack busily taking polaroids of Beatrice and Sharon. The latter had taken to being photographed like a pro: pouting and posing for the camera as if she'd been doing it all her life. 'What's this all for?' Travis asked Jack as the demon examined the results with a satisfied expression.

'All part of my master plan,' said Jack, then said to Sharon, 'You're a natural, babe. The camera doesn't just like you, it wants to have your children.'

Beatrice, who was inspecting one of the polaroids of herself, said, in a rather awed tone, 'I'm incredibly beautiful, aren't I?'

'Yeah, babe, you're okay. You'll break hearts and wet seats,' Jack told her.

Travis was mystified. 'Jack, what is this master plan of yours, and am I going to live to regret it?'

'I can't make speculations on your life expectancy, Travis, but if you are still alive when I get this show on the road you sure won't regret it, I promise you.'

Travis felt far from reassured. Then he experienced a flash of alarm when the doorbell sounded yet again.

'You should put a meter on that thing,' said Jack as Travis left to answer it. Standing outside was a tall black man in a uniform. The words 'Express Delivery' were emblazoned in red on his coat pocket and he was holding a large parcel and a clipboard. 'Could you sign for this, mate?' he asked, handing both parcel and clipboard. Travis, signing with the attached pen, asked who it was from. The delivery man suggested he

26

look at the Sender column on the clipboard. Travis did so and felt a thrill of fear when he saw the name Prenderghast Inc.

'It's from Prenderghast,' he told them as he carried the parcel into the kitchen and gingerly laid it on the table. He stared at it apprehensively.

'Well, open it dickwit,' said Jack. 'It's hardly likely to be a bomb. Prenderghast wouldn't be so unsubtle.'

Travis had to agree with Jack, but it was still with some nervousness that he cut the adhesive tape and unwrapped the parcel.

It turned out to contain a dark blue business suit, white shirt, black tie, blue y-fronts, a pair of black shoes and a pair of black socks.

'Pretty weird,' commented Jack.

Travis recognised the clothes. They were his.

They were what he'd been wearing the afternoon he'd confronted Prenderghast in his office all those months ago – though it was only yesterday as far as this world was concerned.

'They're mine,' said Travis as he picked up the jacket and investigated the inside pocket. He pulled out his wallet and opened it. His credit cards and money were all there.

'Well, that was pretty thoughtful of him,' said Jack. 'The question is – why?'

'My thoughts exactly,' said Travis worriedly.

'Can we go now?' pleaded Beatrice.

'Yeah, I guess so,' sighed Travis. He looked at Jack. 'And what are your plans while we're gone?'

'None of your business.'

'I suppose it will involve more expensive phone calls?'

'I told you. I'll pay you back.'

'Yes, sure,' said Travis. 'Okay, ladies, let's go. And please try not to do anything that might draw attention to yourselves. Especially you, Sharon.'

Sharon tried to look innocent and failed completely. 'Don't worry about a thing, Travis. I'll be on my best behaviour.'

I'm doomed, thought Travis.

Chapter Four

Travis decided to travel by tube rather than take his car. Very soon he was regretting this decision.

He took the two women up to St John's Wood tube station; apart from some dodgy moments crossing the roads he had no serious problems until after they reached the station. The pair were amused by the automatic gates and impressed by the escalator but the trouble began when they were on the platform. As a tube train approached along the tunnel with an increasingly loud rumbling sound they reacted badly. Beatrice covered her ears and started screaming, while Sharon adopted an attack position – claws out, teeth bared and snarling like a large and lethal member of the feline family. People standing nearby on the platform reacted by fainting or leaping onto the tracks and running away.

Travis grabbed each woman by an arm and tugged urgently. 'It's okay! Don't be scared!' he yelled over the noise of the approaching train and Beatrice's screaming. When the train emerged from the tunnel and came to a halt Beatrice stopped screaming, to his relief. And seeing there was no apparent danger, Sharon also relaxed.

'Er ... don't mind them,' said Travis to the nearest bemused bystander. 'They're new to London ... er, they're Australians.'

At the latter comment a large, male, back-packer in his early twenties gave Travis a menacing frown. Travis realized that he was probably an Australian too. He hastily ushered the women into the carriage and down to one end where there were few people about. 'Sit down, be quiet and don't do anything embarrassing,' he told them firmly as he took a seat between them.

Sharon relaxed casually in her seat but Beatrice sat stiffly and then tightly gripped Travis's hand when the train began to move. Sitting opposite Sharon was a suited, middle-aged businessman with a briefcase on his lap and a copy of the *Daily Mail* in his hands. He had checked out Beatrice and Sharon as they'd sat down and then returned his attention to his newspaper, but now kept casting what he presumed to be surreptitious glances at Sharon.

'How long do we have to be in this noisy beast?' Beatrice asked Travis.

'Not long. We have to change onto another one a few stops away and then we'll be there soon after.'

'Good,' said Beatrice. 'I don't like this.'

'Join the club. A lot of people in this city have to endure this at least twice a day, and it's even worse during the rush hour when people are either going to or returning from work.'

'Work? What's that?'

'Something I'd prefer not to think about,' he said. But he couldn't help thinking about his job. He could only put off Martin for so long. He was going to have to tell him *something* before the day was over. But what?

Travis was then distracted by the businessman sitting opposite. He was staring at Sharon and had gone red in the face. Travis then noticed the specific direction in which the man was staring at Sharon. He glanced at Sharon and saw that her sprawling posture had caused her short skirt to ride up high on her thighs. Then he remembered Sharon's lack of underwear. He could imagine only too well the view that the businessman was receiving. It would be like watching *Basic Instinct* with your finger on the 'Pause' button. No wonder that the briefcase on his lap had developed an obvious tilt.

'Sharon, stop showing yourself!' Travis hissed urgently in Sharon's ear.

'What do you mean?'

'You're showing yourself! Stop it!'

'But you said . . . Oh, please yourself.'

The businessman's jaw suddenly dropped and his eyes went very wide with alarm. Travis glanced again at Sharon and saw why. No matter how spectacular the view of Sharon the businessman opposite had been receiving before, it couldn't compare to what he was seeing now within Sharon's skirt. Absolutely nothing.

Sharon had vanished, leaving just her empty shirt and skirt behind. 'Sharon, what are you doing?' he whispered. 'Come back at once!'

'Make up your mind,' came her exasperated voice from thin air. 'You just told me to stop showing myself.'

The man's jaw dropped even further. Travis didn't like the colour he'd gone. He was afraid the man was about to have a heart attack.

'I didn't mean for you to stop showing *all* of yourself!' he cried, 'just a specific bit! Please reappear!'

'Oh, alright,' she muttered, and popped back into view. The man opposite whimpered.

'Good,' sighed Travis. 'Now put your knees together and pull down your skirt.'

'You want me to take my skirt off?' she asked. 'Why?'

'No, not off . . . *down*. Like this . . .' He grabbed the hem of her skirt and pulled it down over her legs. Sharon gave him a puzzled look.

'Why'd you do that?' she asked, puzzled.

'I'll tell you later.'

The train was pulling into Baker Street. The businessman lurched to his feet and staggered quickly to the doors. Travis had a hunch this was not his usual stop. He looked around. No one else seemed to have witnessed Sharon's brief disappearance, but then most hardened Underground users were used to seeing all manner of bizarre sights.

'From now on, stay visible and keep your legs together,' he told Sharon sternly.

'You're strange, Travis,' said Sharon, though she obediently put her knees together.

'I know,' he sighed. 'And I'm getting stranger by the second . . .'

*

'Heather? Hi, it's Martin Shulman . . .'

'Oh, hello, Martin! How are you?' Heather pressed Save and Return on her terminal and settled back in her chair.

'Fine. Look, sorry to bother you at work . . .'

'No problem. Nice to speak to you again . . .'

'It's just that I'm worried about Travis . . .'

'You're not the only one,' she told him.

'He's acting very strangely,' said Shulman.

'You can say that again,' she sighed.

'You know all about the Prenderghast assignment, don't you?'

'Yes, I've heard nothing *but* recently.'

'Well, the deadline for the story is today but Travis told me he might have to postpone it. That's really out of the question. I've tried calling him back but all I get is this rude American answering his phone who keeps telling me to . . . well, frankly, to fuck off. Do you know who he is?'

'No,' said Heather, 'I don't. I called round to his flat this morning and there was a very attractive young woman in his kitchen. And wearing his dressing-gown. I didn't see any man. And Travis was acting very odd. He also said the woman was his cousin. From Australia.' Heather gave a hollow laugh. 'If she was Australian I'm a Martian. And as for being his cousin . . . well, no way.'

'So who do you think she is?' asked Shulman.

'No idea. But it gets weirder. I called his friend Stephen, who lives near by, and this cousin from Australia was news to him as well. He said he'd drop in on Travis and check her out. Then he called me back later and said there were now *two* women in Travis's kitchen. And at first he tried to tell Stephen that they were *both* his cousins. Then Travis gave him a different story – that they were both involved in the Prenderghast business . . .'

'Prenderghast?!' exclaimed Shulman. 'In what way?'

'He didn't elaborate, but he strongly hinted to Stephen that they were in some kind of danger from Prenderghast and were hiding out in his flat as a result.'

31

There was silence on the other end of the line for a few moments. Then Shulman said, 'I don't like the sound of this. I'm going round to see Travis right now.'

'I'll join you,' said Heather. 'I want to get to the bottom of this as well. And if I find out he's getting up to something with either of his so-called cousins I'm going to punch his lights out!'

They changed at Green Park from the Jubilee Line onto the Piccadilly Line. Knightsbridge was only two stops away and they reached it, to Travis's relief, without any further incident, though he noticed that Sharon couldn't help but attract attention. The beautiful Beatrice drew her fair share of appreciative glances too, but the truly exotic-looking Sharon was a magnet to men and women alike. Travis felt he might as well be carrying a large sign saying: 'Danger! Visiting Succubus!'

They emerged from the Knightsbridge exit that directly faced Harrods. The security men raised their eyebrows when they saw the bare-footed Sharon but no one obstructed them as they entered the store. Both of the women were quickly captivated by the lavish surroundings of the exclusive store as Travis led them through it. They liked the Eygptian Room but were especially impressed by the Fine Jewellery Room and Beatrice immediately demanded that Travis buy her a silver necklace that caught her attention. He told her that unfortunately it was a little out of his price range – by some several hundred pounds. He had to tell the same thing to Sharon when she was similarly drawn to another expensive bauble. Both of them regarded him with ominous annoyance so he took them into the Food Hall, correctly assuming that their-ever present appetites would prove a distraction.

He bought a few items – Italian sausages, cheeses, quiche, a couple of bottles of good Italian wine – promising them that they would have a really good picnic when they returned to his flat. They then asked to be guided to the nearest Ladies toilet which Travis proceeded to do. He waited impatiently outside, nervous at letting them out of his sight for even a couple of minutes.

A stream of women, some with small children, entered and left as he waited. At one point the door swung open but no one emerged. He thought nothing more of it until Beatrice appeared. He saw that she was carrying Sharon's skirt and shirt over her arm. Alarm bells started to ring. 'Where's Sharon?' he demanded.

'Oh, she's gone exploring,' said Beatrice airily.

'Exploring? You mean she's wondering around the place *invisible*?' he asked, a falling elevator feeling developing in the pit of his stomach.

'Mmmm, yes. She wants to have a bit of fun.'

'Fun?' repeated Travis weakly. 'What kind of fun?'

In the distance he heard a woman scream.

He guessed, bleakly, that Sharon had started having her fun.

When Heather arrived at Travis's flat, Martin Shulman was already there. A lean, balding man in his early forties, he was kneeling in front of the door and yelling something through the letterbox.

'What's happening?' she asked.

He turned and looked up at her, his face flushed with anger. 'Oh, hello, Heather. I don't know about Travis and the women but that foul-mouthed American bastard is definitely in there. And he's refusing to let me in.' Shulman got to his feet and simultaneously rang the doorbell while pounding on the door with his other hand. 'Open the door at once!'

Heather tapped him on the shoulder and showed him a key. 'Allow me,' she said. He stepped aside and she unlocked the front door. The hallway was empty.

Shulman said, 'Better let me go in first. That Yank sounded a little crazy. He might be dangerous.' Shulman warily entered. Heather, filled with curiosity, followed him. First they checked the living room and then the kitchen. Both rooms were empty. Heather gave a start when Shulman suddenly yelled, 'Come on and show yourself, you bastard! I know you're in here!'

They listened. Then they heard wings flapping. They looked at each other. 'Does Travis own a parrot?' Shulman asked her.

'Not that I know of,' Heather replied. 'But then I didn't know he had cousins in Australia.'

'Maybe the bird belongs to one of them . . .'

'You couldn't bring a foreign bird in through Customs. So that means they're definitely not from overseas . . .' She paused then went to the kitchen table. There were a number of polaroid photographs spread out upon it. 'Look at these.' Shulman joined her at the table. She pointed at one of the photos. 'That's the one I met here this morning. The other one I've never seen before.'

Shulman cleared his throat. 'They're . . . er, certainly *striking* young women.'

'Aren't they just,' she replied, witheringly. Then she sniffed the air. 'I smell cigarette smoke. Travis doesn't smoke.'

Shulman sniffed as well and said, 'Someone has been. And recently. Let's check out the rest of the flat . . .'

The bedroom was empty, as was the bathroom. But they did hear the sound of flapping wings again. 'There's a back way out of here, isn't there?' he asked.

She nodded. 'The fire exit at the end of the hallway. It leads onto outside stairs that go down to the garden.'

They opened the exit door and went out onto the landing. There was no one in the garden. 'The sod must have done a runner out this way,' said Shulman, peering around. 'Probably long gone by now.'

'But who was he? And where is Travis, and his . . . cousins?'

'That's what I'd like to know. Time is running out. I *need* that Prenderghast story!'

After thoroughly searching the entire flat they returned to the kitchen, wondering what to do next. They both jumped

34

when the phone began to ring. 'This had better be Travis,' said Shulman as he snatched it up. 'Travis . . . ?' Then he frowned. 'Jack? No, this is not Jack! Who the hell is Jack? And who the hell are you?' After a pause, Shulman said, 'Arnie? Arnie who?'

Disappointed that it wasn't Travis, Heather went to the refrigerator, hoping that Travis had some orange juice in there. She opened the door, looked in . . . and screamed.

It seemed that all hell was breaking loose in the Fine Jewellery Room. Women were screaming and security guards were racing towards it from all directions. Travis feared the worse. He looked enquiringly at Beatrice but she merely gave him an enigmatic, and infuriating, little smile.

Then, out of the corner of his eye, he saw a cluster of glittery, silver objects flying through the air at waist-height level towards him. Before he could register what they were they swiftly disappeared into his Harrods Food Hall bag. There was a metallic clatter and the bag immediately grew heavier. 'What the . . . ?' Then he gasped as something dug hard into his ribs.

'Just act normal, Travis,' he heard Sharon say softly near his ear, then she laughed.

'What have you done?' he demanded.

'I suggest we all head towards the exit,' she told him. 'And fast.'

Chapter Five

'Here, have some more scotch,' said Shulman. He took the glass from her, poured some scotch into it and handed it back. She took another grateful swallow.

'I still can't believe it,' said Heather, shakily. 'What on Earth was a *bat* doing in Travis's fridge?'

'Haven't a clue,' said Shulman. 'And what a bloody ugly thing it was too.'

'Dreadful creature!' she agreed. 'I just hope it doesn't come back.'

'It must be hiding somewhere in the flat. All the windows are shut.'

'I think Travis is having some kind of breakdown,' she said, having another swallow of scotch.

'I hate to agree with you but I'm beginning to think the same,' said Shulman. 'But what mystifies me is how quickly it's happened. He was all right yesterday. I mean, it's true his working methods have always been kind of unorthodox but he's always come through with the goods. What about you? Have you noticed anything unusual about him recently?'

She frowned. 'Not really. He's never been exactly *normal* but he was his usual self. He did stand me up in a restaurant last night, but he's done that before when he's been in the thick of an assignment.'

'It's all tied up with this Prenderghast thing,' said Shulman. 'Something happened when he saw Prenderghast yesterday.'

'You don't think . . .? No, not Travis.' She took her head. 'What is it?'

'I shouldn't have even thought it,' she said. 'Not about Travis.'

'Go on. You can tell me,' he urged. 'It won't go any further.'

'Well . . .' she lowered her voice. 'What if Prenderghast *bribed* Travis?'

Shulman looked shocked. 'Travis take a bribe? No, never!'

'He *might* have,' she said, defensively. 'Prenderghast is fabulously wealthy. What if he offered Travis something so . . . so *valuable* he couldn't say no?'

Shulman considered this. 'No, I've never had any doubts about Travis's integrity. He wouldn't accept a cash bribe, no matter how big.'

'What if it wasn't money?' she asked him and gave him a meaningful look.

He frowned. 'I don't follow . . .'

'What if Prenderghast bribed him with these *women*?' She picked up a couple of the polaroid photographs from the table and waved them under Shulman's nose. 'His so-called cousins from Australia? What if Prenderghast gave them to Travis as sex slaves?'

He stared at the photographs of the two stunningly beautiful women. 'Noooooo. . . ,' he said slowly, but there was now doubt in his voice.

'I still can't believe you did what you did!' said Travis heatedly. 'You could have got me arrested!'

Sharon didn't answer. Beatrice said, 'Travis, stop it. You're making a spectacle of yourself.'

'*Me*?' *I'm* making a spectacle of myself! That's a laugh!'

'Please, you're embarrassing me,' said Beatrice and turned away from him.

'*I'm* embarrassing *you*!? You . . . you . . .' And then, abruptly, the coin of reality dropped and he became aware of his situation. They were in a carriage on the Piccadilly Line. It was fairly crowded, there were no empty seats so they were standing by the doors. Travis looked round. He was the focus of attention. Several pairs of eyes regarded with a mixture curiosity, alarm and pity. The reason was clear. He had been haranguing Sharon since getting in the carriage. The problem was that Sharon was still invisible. Her skirt and shirt were in the carrier bag he was holding, along with the cheeses, the quiche, the bottles of wine and about £50,000 pounds worth of stolen silver jewellery. 'Shit,' he muttered as he felt his face go bright red.

'Where are we going now?' Beatrice asked him over her shoulder.

'I don't know . . . Yes, I do. To my club. I need a drink.'

'You need a psychiatrist, mate,' said a tough-looking young man standing nearby. 'You're a raving loony.'

Travis gave him a sheepish grin and cursed Sharon under his breath.

Suddenly the young man gave a grunt of pain and clutched his groin. He looked round suspiciously but there was clearly no one close enough to have hit him. He glared at Travis, and immediately cried out again as Sharon did something unpleasant to his groin area. The man looked worried now and started to move down the carriage away from Travis. Travis decided Sharon had her uses after all.

They got off at Leicester Square and he led Beatrice and the invisible Sharon up through China Town to Old Compton Street where his club, The Soho Centre, was located. At the entrance he paused and said firmly, 'When we go in, I want you, Beatrice, to take Sharon's clothes into the Ladies toilets. Sharon, you will go with her, put on the clothes and reappear. Understood?' Beatrice nodded and Sharon muttered, 'Yes.'

He used his smart card to open the door and they entered. At the reception desk he signed in both Beatrice and Sharon, using fictional surnames. The receptionist, whose name was Cathy, looked puzzled. 'Where's your other guest, Mr Thomson?'

'She'll be along later,' Travis told her. He led the way up the stairs to the main bar. The club catered mainly to media types: journalists, advertising people and a smattering of TV producers and writer types. At this time of the day it wasn't very busy and Travis was relieved to see that there were only a couple of other members in the bar. Travis recognised the horror writer, Harry Adam Knight, who always seemed to be drunk, no matter what time of the day it was. Today was no exception – the writer was perched precariously on a barstool with his eyes closed. Travis wondered once again when the writer did any actual writing. He ordered three glasses of red wine, then guided Beatrice, and Sharon, to the Ladies. He handed Beatrice the bag. 'All right, girls, you know what to do. And no more tricks, Sharon.'

He went back to the bar, swallowed his entire glass of wine in one gulp and ordered another. Then he asked the barman, whose name was Tod, for a phone. When it came he rang his own flat. Jack answered. 'Arnie?'

'No, it's me, Travis. Just checking to see what new disasters have occurred. I suppose my phone bill is as long as a phone number. In the Outer Hebrides.'

'Nah, not even close. Don't give it a thought. What have you been up to?'

'Oh, nothing much.' He turned away from the bar and lowered his voice. 'Sharon only robbed the Fine Jewellery Room at Harrods. We were lucky to get out of the place . . .'

'Good for her,' said Jack. 'How much is the haul worth?'

'About fifty thousand pounds, give or take a few thousand.'

'Hmmm, not bad. A good fence will give us at least half that.'

'A good *fence*? I'm not selling the stuff, I'm going to post it back to Harrods anonymously.'

'Jeez, you can be a klutz at times. You need the cash. So do I. I need some seeding money.'

'I am sending the jewellery back,' said Travis firmly. 'And what do you need *seeding* money for?'

'You'll find out. Oh, you had visitors . . .'

'Who?' he asked anxiously.

'One of them was your old lady . . .'

'My *mother?!*' yelped Travis.

'No, you jerk, your bimbo, Heather. And a bald guy. A real dork.'

'That must have been Martin, my boss. Did they see you?'

'Sort of,' said Jack.

'What do you mean – sort of?'

'They caught me off-guard so I stupidly hid in the icebox again. Your bimbo opened the door.'

'Oh no,' groaned Travis.

'Great set of lungs, your girl. My ears are still ringing.'

'So they both saw you.'

'Relax. They thought I was a bat. And a bloody ugly one at that, according to the dork.'

'Then what happened?' Travis asked wearily.

'I hid out in the bedroom on top of the wardrobe. Listened to what they had to say?'

'Which was?'

'You sure you want to hear this?'

'Just tell me.'

'Well, your ever-loving babe and your dork loyal boss have come to a conclusion as to why you're acting so weird . . .'

'Which is?'

'They think Prenderghast bribed you.'

'They don't!' cried Travis, appalled.

'They sure do,' said Jack with a chuckle. 'And here's the really funny bit . . . they think Beatrice and Sharon are the main part of the bribe.'

'They don't!' cried Travis again, even more appalled.

'They think they're your sex slaves.'

'No!' he cried, his level of being appalled reaching its peak.

'I'm afraid so. Your girl is now on the warpath. She's looking for you. And for your sake I hope she's not the type who's into wearing a lot of rings on her right hand.'

'Heather wouldn't . . .' he began, and paused. Oh yes she would.

'I've got to go now,' Jack said. 'Need to keep the line clear

40

for Arnie. Good luck, pal. You're going to need it.' Jack chuckled again and hung up.

Travis hung up as well and sighed. He turned back to the bar, wondering what he was going to say to Heather when he next encountered her. And how on earth could either she or Martin think he could have taken a bribe from Prenderghast? And in the form of Beatrice and Sharon? As sex slaves? Well, actually, the idea wasn't *that* too far-fetched if you thought about it. Speaking of whom . . .

He looked anxiously towards the entrance to the bar. Where had they got too? If they'd done a runner he'd . . . he'd . . . he didn't know what he'd do. But just then the two of them came through the doorway, both grinning and looking pleased with themselves. 'It's so *good* to see you again, Sharon,' he told her pointedly as she sat down beside him. She stuck her tongue out at him then turned and smiled at Tod the barman. Tod was regarding her with rapt attention. And Travis knew that he was gay.

Beatrice sipped her wine then looked around the bar. 'What is this place, Travis?'

Travis thought her question over. 'Well, it's rather like a tavern. But it's not open to the public like a tavern. It's a private club. You pay money to be a member.'

'You don't have to pay to go into a tavern, do you?' asked Beatrice.

'No.'

'Then why do you pay to drink here when you could simply go to a tavern?'

'Because . . .' he said and faltered. 'Because . . . because it has attractions that taverns don't have.'

'Such as?'

'Erm, a good restaurant . . . a pleasant atmosphere . . .'

'Is that all?'

'Well, to be honest you can avoid the people who usually drink in taverns.'

'Oh, I see,' she said, nodding. 'Commoners, you mean.

41

Riff-raff. People like this servant here.' She indicated Tod with her glass.

'Not exactly,' Travis said uneasily. Tod had been sufficiently diverted from Sharon by the conversation to give Beatrice a dirty look to which she was completely oblivious. Tod redirected the dirty look at him. He decided it was time for a change of subject. 'Hand me the bag, please,' he said, referring to the Harrods bag which she'd placed on the other side of her stool.

'Why?' she asked, even as she did as he asked.

'Just checking,' he said as he peered into it. Yes, all the silver pieces appeared to be there. He had been struck by the thought that the two women may have hidden a few of them on their persons while in the toilet.

'I thought I'd find you here,' said a voice behind him. A voice he knew well.

It was Heather's voice.

Shit. He turned and forced a smile. Heather and Martin were standing there. Both looked angry. 'Oh, hello,' he said. 'Like a drink?'

'No, thanks,' snapped Heather. 'Been showing your *cousins* the sights, have you?'

'Er . . .'

'I don't believe it,' said Martin. 'You've got a crucial deadline today and yet here you are drinking in your club in the middle of the afternoon! Have you gone crazy?'

'Er, are you sure you won't have a drink?' He turned round and said to Tod, 'Two more House Reds, please.'

'Addressing the riff-raff, are you, Mr Thomson?' said Tod with a sneer.

'Look, I'm sor . . .' He was interrupted by a violent prod in his back. It was Heather's forefinger.

'Forget the wine,' she told him. 'And forget all that rubbish about these two *tarts* being your cousins. We want the truth.'

'What's a tart?' asked Beatrice, suspiciously.

'It's a small pastry with a jam filling,' Travis told her.

'Don't try that Miss Innocence act with me!' Heather

42

exploded at Beatrice. 'Sitting there in *my* clothes with your ''Butter Wouldn't Melt in My Pussy'' expression!'

'Heather, you don't understand . . .' pleaded Travis – to no avail.

'Oh, I understand all right, Travis Thomson!' she cried. 'I understand only too well! You sold out to Prenderghast in return for the sexual favours of these two tramps!'

'What's a tramp?' asked Beatrice.

'Travis, your woman-friend is starting to annoy me,' said Sharon, ominously.

Heather turned to her. 'And what part of Australia are you supposed to be from? Tasmania as well? You look rather like a Tasmanian devil!'

Uh-oh, bad move, thought Travis. Sharon hissed at Heather, causing her to flinch. Travis put a restraining hand on Sharon's shoulder and murmured, 'Easy, easy . . .' To his relief, Sharon didn't launch herself at Heather, who was now looking very uncomfortable.

'Is it true, Travis?' demanded Martin. 'Have you sold out to Prenderghast? Is that why you haven't delivered the story?'

'No, I haven't sold out, Martin, and I'm disappointed that you think I could be bribed.'

'Then where's the story?'

'There's a problem . . . I can't explain right now.'

'Well, you'd better, Travis, or I'll have no choice but to ask for your resignation,' Martin told him grimly.

'You don't mean that!' Travis exclaimed.

'I'm afraid I do. Either you give me a satisfactory explanation or you lose your job . . .'

Before Travis could say anything one of the club managers, Chris, entered the bar and came over to their group. He was a smooth, good-looking man in his early thirties. Travis wasn't sure but suspected that he and Tod were lovers. 'Everything alright in here? I thought I heard raised voices . . .'

'Everything is fine, Chris,' lied Travis.

'Good, good,' Chris beamed, seemingly unaware of the

tension in the air. Then he suddenly looked down and frowned. 'Mr Thomson, you know we don't have a dress code in this establishment but there *are* limits.'

Travis had no idea what he was talking about but guessed it meant more trouble heading his way. He was quickly proved right. 'Sorry?'

Chris pointed down. 'Your guest is bare-footed. Unless she puts some shoes on I must ask her to leave. *And* her feet are filthy.'

Travis looked. He'd entirely forgotten that Sharon wasn't wearing any shoes. And Chris was right – her feet were filthy. 'Er, she doesn't have any shoes,' he said.

'I'm sorry then, but you must ask your guest to leave the premises,' he told Travis.

'Hah!' laughed Heather.

'Is this idiot throwing me out?' Sharon asked Travis.

'I'm afraid so. But we'll come with you . . .'

Sharon threw the remaining wine in her glass into Chris's face. 'Stupid dolt,' she snarled at him.

Chris, with wine dripping from his face and onto his white shirt, reacted first with surprise, then fury. 'You *bitch*!' he cried at Sharon. Sharon's response was to stand up and let loose a haymaker that lifted him off his feet and then flattened him on his back.

A shocked silence followed. Then, from the floor, Chris groaned, 'Tod, call the police . . .'

That was bad enough, thought Travis, but what made it even worse was the fact he was in the possession of a Harrod's bag containing at least fifty thousand pounds worth of stolen silver jewellery.

Chapter Six

At precisely 10pm, in an alley off a square in London's East End, a chicken exploded. This event profoundly surprised brothers Barry and Nigel who were lurking in the alley at the time, as the alley, until then, had been an entirely chicken-free zone. The chicken – a rooster – had suddenly materialised in mid-air before spectacularly detonating with a brilliant flash of fire.

Barry and Nigel Simmons were in the alley, peering over the top of a portabin filled with the leftovers from the adjacent Indian restaurant, because they were hoping to mug somebody that night. Preferably someone old or Asian. An old Asian would have suited them perfectly. The Simmons brothers could have been identical twins even though they were not in reality. They had round, shaven heads, broad shoulders and beer bellies, but despite their physical similarities they differed as far as their personalities were concerned: Barry was stupidly vicious while Nigel was viciously stupid.

While they were still reacting with stunned amazement at the exploding chicken, something even more bizarre happened. In the middle of the cloud of singed feathers two men suddenly appeared. One was tall and one was short. The shorter one had a walking stick. Both were dressed in strange-looking black clothes and both wore cloaks. The taller man was coughing and sneezing. He took out a handkerchief, wiped his mouth and then said, 'Dash it all, Damion, but was that chicken absolutely necessary?'

'It was crucial, sire, I assure you,' said the smaller one.

The tall man stared around and Barry and Nigel quickly ducked out of sight. 'Where are we?'

'If my incantations were all correct, Prince Valerie,

somewhere in a city called London. It's where Travis resides.'

'So he's nearby?'

'Well, possibly.'

'What do you mean – *possibly*?'

'It's a big city. Much bigger than any city on Samella.'

'Couldn't you have put us right in his immediate vicinity?'

'Sorry, sire. Beyond the scope of my powers. All I know is that we're in the right city an in the same day that he and others arrived here. Give or take a day.'

'Can't you sniff out the whereabouts of your treacherous succubus?'

'I've tried. She must be out of range.'

'Damion, I'm beginning to feel rather pissed off with you.'

'Sorry, sire.'

None of this conversation made any sense to Barry and Nigel. Barry whispered to Nigel, 'Who are those nutters?'

'I dunno,' Nigel whispered back. 'Never seen them before. You think they're poofs?'

'They sure look like poofs. And they talk funny so they must be foreigners.'

'You think they might be Paki poofs?'

'Nah, they're not Pakis,' said Barry, 'but I do think they're poofs. The little one called the tall geezer "Valerie".'

'What are we gonna do?'

'Let's take 'em. You sort out the short one and I'll do "Valerie". Know what I mean?'

'Right.' Then he said, 'Barry?'

'Yeah?'

'Where did that chicken come from? And what made it blow up?'

'*They* must have done it somehow. This pair of foreign poofdah sex perverts. Let's get 'em.'

Barry and Nigel stepped out from behind the portabin. Both produced switch-blades and simultaneously pressed the

46

release buttons. The 'clicks' caused the two strangers to turn and face them.

'Hello, what have we here?' said the tall man, unconcernedly.

'A pair of common cut-throats, by the look of them,' commented the smaller man. '*Very* common.'

Barry and Nigel continued to advance on the pair. 'You're spot-on there, runt,' growled Barry. 'And after we've cut your throats we're gonna cut off your balls, know what I mean?'

'Those are awfully small blades,' said the tall man and, in a blur of movement, produced a sword from under his cape. 'As you can see, my own weapon is considerably larger.'

Barry and Nigel came to a sudden stop. They exchanged a worried look.

'Drop your silly little blades,' ordered the tall man, whose eyes were now glowing red in a very off-putting way, 'before I run you both through on the spot.'

Two switch-blades simultaneously hit the floor of the alley. 'We didn't mean you no harm,' said Barry quickly. 'We was just havin' some fun, know what I mean,' he added, 'Sir.'

'Destroy them, sire,' said the smaller man, contemptuously.

'Let's not be too hasty,' said the man with the red eyes. And the sword.

'Yeah, mate, let's not be hasty,' agreed Barry, his voice rising by an octave.

'Yeah,' seconded Nigel, who was scared and very confused.

'As you may have surmised,' said the tall man, 'we are strangers to your fair city . . .'

'Er, welcome to London . . . sir,' said Barry.

'Thank you. And as strangers we could do with a couple of guides and all-purpose helpers.'

'We don't need these fools,' muttered the smaller one.

The tall one turned to him. 'I disagree. I think these two, sturdy dullards will be of use.'

47

'Oh, we're sturdy all right!' said Barry.

'And dullards,' added Nigel. He wasn't sure what a dullard was but like Barry he was anxious to please the tall man.

'With their help we will be able to track down Travis and the others so much faster,' the tall man told the smaller man.

'Oh, I suppose so,' said the latter, but not sounding convinced.

To Barry and Nigel's profound relief the tall man sheathed his sword. 'Good. That's settled then. Now I could do with a drink . . .'

'Great!' said Barry. 'We'll take you down to the Tug and Pullet. I could do with a few beers myself.'

The tall man moved towards him. 'It wasn't beer I had in mind,' he said and smiled at Barry, showing his teeth.

'And that's when the policewoman, WPC Westland, got that nasty bite on the leg?' asked the police psychiatrist.

'I guess so, but it wasn't me,' said Travis. 'It was probably Sharon.'

'Sharon? Oh, yes, the *succubus*. The police on the scene don't recall seeing this other woman.'

'No, Dave. That's because she would have been invisible by then.'

The psychiatrist peered at his notebook and nodded. 'Oh, yes. She's the invisible woman. But you do admit hitting the policeman, PC Wellman?'

'It was more of a shove . . . I panicked.'

'And you hit the club bouncer.'

Travis sighed. 'Yes.'

'And the club manager?'

'I was trying to get out the place. They were trying to stop me.'

'Why were you so anxious to leave? Surely the matter could have been sorted out calmly and rationally.'

'Sharon started the violence. And she's far from being calm and rational at the best of times.'

The psychiatrist nodded. 'Ah, yes, this Sharon again. Who no one saw.'

Travis lit another cigarette and said impatiently, 'Plenty of people saw her. She was the reason the police were called. She decked Chris, the manager, after he told her to leave. Because she wasn't wearing any shoes.' Travis sighed again as he realized how absurd all this sounded. Good ol' Dave was clearly convinced he was completely out of his tree. Trying to tell him the truth had been a serious mistake. He should have made up some story. But what? He could hardly have told him he had been desperate to get out of the club because he was holding a Harrods bag containing a large amount of stolen silver. Thank goodness the bag had disappeared in all the confusion. He guessed Sharon must have taken it. Or Beatrice.

'But this Sharon wasn't there when the police arrived,' pointed out Dave. 'And the other young woman in your company, the, er, *princess*. She couldn't be found afterwards either. Did she turn invisible as well?'

'No. She just has this uncanny knack to walk through a hail of shit and come out completely unscathed. Probably something to do with her royal genes.'

'And where do you think these two women are now?'

Travis shrugged. 'No idea. And to tell the truth, I'm rather worried about them. They're newcomers to a world that is totally alien to them. I'm sure they won't be able to find their way back to my flat. And they don't have any money.' *Only about fifty thousand pounds worth of Harrods jewellery*, he thought wryly.

The 'call-me-Dave' psychiatrist leaned back in his chair and regarded Travis in a sympathetic way that really got up Travis's nose. 'You do realize you need help, don't you, Travis?'

'True bloody right I do,' said Travis.

'You're going to need a lot of therapy and counselling. And I think a course of anti-depressants is also called for.'

'The anti-depressants I'm all for,' Travis told him. 'But you can stuff your therapy and counselling.'

Dave shook his head sadly. 'This attitude of yours is not helping, Travis. You must co-operate with me if we're going to uncover the pressures that drove you into this fantasy world of yours.'

'Everything I told you is true. If you won't believe me that's your problem.'

'Travis, all this talk of demons, princesses . . . invisible women . . . how *can* I believe it?' Dave asked him.

'With great difficulty,' admitted Travis wearily. Just then the door to the interview room opened. Travis expected to see another police officer entering but there was no one there. The door swung shut again. The officer standing by the door frowned and opened it again. He looked outside then said to Dave, 'Funny. No one there.'

'Must have been the wind,' said Dave and returned his attention to Travis. 'Travis, I'm afraid I'm going to recommend that you remain in custody for the time being. In my opinion, in your current mental state you represent a danger both to yourself and to others . . .'

It was only when he felt a presence brush by him that Travis realized that Sharon was in the room. He tensed, unsure whether to be relieved or worried. What was she going to do?

He soon found out.

'I am sorry, Travis, but that's the situation as I . . .' Dave suddenly stopped, a surprised expression on his face. He looked down at his lap. 'What. . . ?' he exclaimed. Then he gave a shudder. 'Ooohhh,' he said.

'You all right, sir?' asked the police constable at the door.

Dave stared at him, then at Travis and then down at his lap again. 'What's happening? I don't understand. Oooooo . . .'

Travis now had a good idea what was going on. He couldn't help smiling. Dave tried to rise from his chair and collapsed back into it. From the look on his face he was profoundly enjoying what he was experiencing – Sharon was,

50

after all, a supernatural expert at her job – despite his astonishment. 'Ooooo . . . ahhhh . . . oooooo!' said Dave.

'Are you *sure* you're all right, sir?' asked the PC again. He made to move towards Dave but the psychiatrist held up a hand.

'No . . . Ooooo . . . stay where . . . you . . . are!'

'But, sir,' said the PC, worriedly, 'What should I do? Should I go and fetch help?'

'No . . . Oooo! . . . No!'

'But . . . but . . .'

Travis watched as Dave's face became contorted with intense pleasure. The veins stood out on his neck and threw his head back. 'Yes . . . yes! . . . *yes!* . . . *Oh, bloody hell . . . YES!! YES!!!!*' Then his whole body slumped forward. He looked completely drained and his eyes were unfocussed. Travis grinned at him and held out his pack of cigarettes to him. 'Do you smoke afterwards as a rule, Dave?' he asked.

'Wha . . . wha . . . what happened?' gasped Dave.

'You should know,' Travis told him.

'Sir, I don't understand . . . what happened to you?' asked the concerned PC.

'Tell him, *Dave*,' said Travis, enjoying himself.

'I don't . . . know,' said the psychiatrist as he fiddled with his lap. Travis presumed he was doing his zipper back up.

'I think Dave had what could be described as an ''out-of-trousers-experience'',' said Travis to the PC. 'Right Dave?'

Dave gave him a stricken look. 'What did you do to me?' he demanded.

'Hey, don't look at me!' protested Travis. 'I didn't lay a finger on you and you know that.'

'But it must have been you . . . *somehow*. There's no one else here apart from PC Watson!'

'That's not exactly true,' said Travis as he felt Sharon brush by him again as she emerged from under the desk. 'You've just encountered Sharon, that succubus I told you about.'

'Rubbish!' cried Dave. 'She's just a figment of your delirious imagination!'

'Sharon?' asked Travis. 'You want to say anything?'

'Sure. The man's a dolt,' came Sharon's voice from beside Travis. 'But he does have a sizeable prodder.'

Dave gawped at Travis. 'You must be a ventriloquist . . .'

'I can't throw a ball, much less my voice.'

'Sir, what's going on?' asked the PC, plaintively.

'Show them, Sharon,' said Travis.

'Okay.' Sharon immediately popped into view in all her naked glory. She perched herself on the edge of the desk, leaned towards Dave and tickled him under the chin. 'You're quite a mouthful, Dave,' she said, with approval.

There was a loud thump. Travis turned. The PC was lying on the floor. He had passed out. Travis turned back to Dave and grinned at him. 'She's not bad for a mere figment of my delirious imagination, is she Dave?'

The psychiatrist was staring with horror at Sharon who was now running her fingers through what remained of his hair. 'This can't be happening,' he moaned. 'I've been hypnotised . . . it's the only possible explanation.'

Travis sighed. 'I know how you feel but I'm afraid you're going to have to face the truth. Sharon is as real as you or me. Sharon, show him how real you can be.'

Sharon jumped nimbly down from the desk and then bent down and plucked Dave out of his chair. She shook him violently back and forth for a short time, then kissed him on the mouth. She dropped him back into his chair.

'Getting the message?' Travis asked him.

'I've lost my mind,' said Dave feebly. 'I'm as insane as you.'

'Remember, we're not comfortable with the word "insane", Dave,' Travis told him with a patronising smile. 'We would prefer to describe you as being in a very disturbed state.'

Dave gave a moan of despair. Sharon giggled.

'Now,' said Travis, 'I'm going to tell you what I want you to do . . .'

Chapter Seven

An unnatural silence descended upon the bar of the Tug and
Pullet public house. It wasn't the entrance of Barry and Nigel
that produced this effect on the assembled patrons but the
appearance of the two men who accompanied the brothers.
The regulars of the Tug and Pullet had never seen anything
like it before, and thus distracted failed to notice that Barry
and Nigel were both looking unusually pale and shaken.

The silence was broken when one of the male regulars
guffawed loudly. And then another young man, shaven-
headed like the brothers, called out, 'Hey, Barry who are your
new girlfriends?'

This produced an outburst of general laughter in the bar.
Barry and Nigel looked uncomfortable. The two long-haired,
oddly dressed strangers looked around disdainfully. Barry
said to the young man who had spoken out, when the laughter
had died down, 'Knock it off, will yer, Gary? These two . . .
gentlemen . . . are the *business*, know what I mean? We're
working for them.'

'You're working for this pair of nonces?' asked the one
called Gary, scornfully. 'Look at them! They look like
they've come straight from some poofdahs' pantomime!'

Barry winced. 'Gary, watch it . . . don't rub them the wrong
way . . .'

'*Rub* them? I wouldn't dare touch them,' sneered Gary.
'I'd probably get a disease.'

'I wish you hadn't said that,' sighed Barry.

The tall man glanced at the smaller one and said, pointing a
finger at Gary, 'Deal with this irritating pustule.'

'With pleasure,' said the smaller one and gesticulated at
Gary.

Gary, automatically presuming an obscene element in the

small man's gesticulations, raised his fist and took a step towards him. 'You little bastard! I'm going to shove your teeth down your backside . . . oink! Oink!'

Gary had lost his grasp – which had never been particularly strong – on the English language because he no longer possessed a human vocal apparatus. This was due to the fact that he was now a small pig.

Once again a rare and unusual silence descended upon the bar of the Tug and Pullet. Finally one of the older regulars observed, 'Now *there's* something you don't see every day.'

'Oink! Oink!' cried Gary as he ran frantically about on the bar room floor.

'I warned you,' Barry told him as people began to back warily away from the pair of decidedly odd strangers.

'Bring the fool back to his previous near-human form,' said the tall one.

The smaller man gesticulated again. There was a flash of light and when it had died away they saw that Gary was his normal self again. He stood there swaying, his face a picture of stark horror. 'Bugger me . . .' he gasped.

'Another time perhaps,' said the tall man as he grasped him by the throat. 'Permit me to introduce myself – I am Prince Valerie, and my companion is called Damion. Do you have any smart comments to make about our names?'

'No . . .' gasped Gary.

'Good,' said Prince Valerie and then threw him across the bar. Gary crashed into the wall, shattering the glass in the greatly-prized framed portrait of the Krays, and collapsed into an inert heap. The regulars of the Tug and Pullet, who held any form of physical violence in high regard, applauded.

Prince Valerie acknowledged the applause with a small bow. 'Thank you. And now I have an announcement to make – I, Prince Valerie, have annexed this establishment and all its inhabitants. You are now my subjects. Kneel!'

The regulars of the Tug and Pullet knelt as one.

'I don't know if I'll be able to do it,' said Dave, still casting nervous glances at Sharon who was reclining across the desk looking bored and suggestively sucking her thumb. 'The charges against you are serious.'

'Oh, I think you'll manage it okay,' said Travis, airily. 'Otherwise you're going to be stuck with Sharon. And I promise you she'll make your life hell. Won't you, Sharon?'

She pulled out her thumb and inspected it. 'Sure,' she said, then resumed sucking.

Dave stared at her. 'I still can't believe this is happening.'

'I know how you feel. It took me quite some time to accept it myself,' said Travis.

'But I'm a rationalist! This goes against my whole world view! I've never believed in the supernatural! And you're telling me that this . . . this . . . *lady* . . . is a *demon*?'

'A succubus, to be correct. She feeds on mortal men's souls, among other things. And it wouldn't surprise me if she hadn't supped on yours while she was . . . servicing you.'

'I only had a nibble,' said Sharon around her thumb.

'I don't believe in the existence of souls,' said Dave.

'Like you don't believe in demons like Sharon here?' asked Travis.

Dave didn't answer.

'Sharon, show him another of your party tricks,' Travis told her.

Sharon nodded and immediately began to shrink. Very soon she was a mere six inches or so in length. Dave's eyes bulged. Then she returned to her normal size and tweaked his cheek. Dave groaned.

There was another groan, this time from the floor. 'He's coming round,' said Dave. Travis said to Sharon, 'Make yourself scarce.' She obediently winked out of sight. Travis and the psychiatrist went over to the fallen constable. The PC's eyes fluttered open. Then he quickly sat up and looked wildly around the room. 'Where is she?' he cried.

'Where's who?' asked Dave as he helped the PC to his feet.

'The woman! The naked woman! The one who just popped out of thin air!'

56

'Calm down, lad,' said Dave soothingly. 'There was no woman here. You had some kind of fit and collapsed. I suggest you visit your doctor and arrange for a full check-up . . .'

'But I *saw* her! And so did you!' The PC got up, pushed past them, went to the desk and peered under it. 'Where did she go?'

'I tell you, there was no woman here, naked or otherwise,' Dave told him. 'You had some sort of hallucination, connected with your fit, I suspect. I suggest you have a brain scan . . .'

The PC ignored him. 'She must have gone outside. Sergeant Potts would have seen her . . .' He headed towards the door. Dave blocked his way. 'Think, lad, before you go out there and make a fool of yourself.'

'What do you mean?' the PC asked suspiciously.

'What do you think it's going to look like if you go out there and start ranting about a naked woman who appeared from nowhere? All you'll achieve is a suspension and an appointment with me for a psychiatric assessment. Think about it.'

The PC did so. Then he said, 'But she was *here*. I know I saw her.'

'Whatever you think you saw it would be wise not to tell anyone else. Right?'

The PC slowly nodded, then he looked at Travis and pointed at him. 'It's all to do with him, isn't it? And now you two are in cohoots, right?'

Dave cleared his throat. 'Mr Thomson has seen the error of his ways and has agreed to voluntarily seek psychiatric help. Therefore I'm going to recommend to the custody officer that the charges be dropped immediately.'

The PC's stare became even more suspicious. 'He's done something to you, hasn't he? While I was out of it something happened between you two. What is he – some kind of hypnotist?'

'Just take my advice, lad, and forget about everything you

think has happened in here tonight. It will be better for all concerned. *You* in particular.'

The PC scowled. 'All right, but I don't like this.'

Dave gripped him manfully by the shoulder. 'Good lad. You won't regret it.' Then he turned to Travis. 'Right, let's go and sort this out.'

'Fine with me,' said Travis. 'Sharon, come on, we're leaving.'

'Right behind you, boss,' came Sharon's disembodied voice, followed by the pitter-patter of bare feet across the floor. The PC made a squeaking sound, then gave a yelp. 'Someone just goosed me!' he cried.

Travis sighed. 'Sharon, behave yourself,' he told her sternly.

'Don't I always?' she replied.

When Travis, accompanied by Dave, went out into the waiting room, after being released on bail, he was surprised to see Beatrice sitting in the waiting room. Then he saw the Harrods bag on her lap and groaned inwardly. She had brought about fifty thousand pounds worth of stolen property into a police station.

When she saw him she gave him a radiantly innocent smile and sprang to her feet. 'How marvellous!' she cried as she hugged him. 'Sharon said she'd get you out and she was right!'

'Yes. Good old Sharon,' he said, gently disengaging himself from her embrace. He was anxious to get out of the station. More to the point, he was anxious to get that Harrods bag out of the station.

'Ahem . . .' said Dave, theatrically. 'And who might this be?'

Travis had forgotten he was there. 'Oh, sorry,' he said to Dave, who was staring at Beatrice with rapt fascination. 'This is Beatrice. *Princess* Beatrice, to be exact. Princess, this is Dave.'

'Oh, yes, the princess,' said Dave. 'Of course. Yes. I hope you're having an enjoyable stay in our world, your highness.'

She regally held out her hand for him to kiss it. After a pause, he kissed it. 'It's certainly been very *interesting* to date, Dave,' she told him. 'This world is completely different to mine.'

'I'm sure it is,' said Dave, still staring at her intensely.

'We'd better go,' said Travis. He turned to Dave and shook his hand. 'Thanks for your help.'

'You know you've turned my entire world upside down,' said Dave.

'Welcome to the club. Goodbye Dave,' he said.

'Yes, goodbye Dave,' said Beatrice.

'And goodbye from me, Dave,' came Sharon's voice from nowhere. Dave flinched.

Travis hurriedly shepherded Beatrice towards the door. 'How did you find me?' he asked her in a low voice.

'We followed you.'

'How? You two were on foot.'

'Sharon followed your smell. She says your smell is very distinctive.'

'Good grief, that's what they used to say about me in school.'

They emerged into the street. Travis had been taken to the West End Central police station which was located near Piccadilly Circus. He hailed a passing black cab. To his amazement the driver didn't claim that he was heading home; that he had left his 'Vacant' sign on by mistake; that he was on his tea break; that he wasn't really a taxi driver but had borrowed the cab from a friend . . . instead he actually agreed to take them to St John's Wood. Profoundly grateful, Travis held the door open for Beatrice, got in after her and then made room for the invisible Sharon. Sharon said, 'Ow! This seat is cold!'

'Shush!' ordered Travis. Thankfully, the driver appeared not to have heard her.

As the cab pulled away from the curb Beatrice reached into

the Harrod bag and produced a silver tiara. She flourished it in front of Travis's nose. 'Isn't this lovely?' she asked.

He shut his eyes and groaned.

'Where have you been all this time?' Jack asked him. Jack was in his study/office and perched next to the fax machine, which was whirring away.

'Part of the time I was in prison,' said Travis as he wearily settled into a chair. He gave Jack the grim details. As he expected, Jack found it all hugely amusing.

'I'm glad you find it so bloody funny,' growled Travis. 'Not only have I lost my girlfriend, I'm pretty certain I'm about to lose my job. And as I'm the one who pays the bills around here it's going to affect *you* as well.'

'Relax. You're going to have a new career.'

'Oh, really,' said Travis, sarcastically. 'And what exactly is this new career of mine?'

'The movie business,' Jack told him. 'We're gonna make a movie.'

Chapter Eight

Travis took another large swallow from his extra large scotch and soda and said to Jack, 'Okay, run that by me again now that I'm becoming anaesthetized. I think I can just about handle it.'

He and Jack were now in the kitchen. The two women were attacking the Harrods food as if it was the first meal they'd had in a decade or two. Jack, perched on the TV set, was smoking a Marlboro.

'It's simple, dickwit,' said Jack. 'We're gonna make a movie. Or to be more accurate, *I* am, with your assistance. And with the babes' help too.'

'You're talking out of an orifice which is not your mouth, though there is a striking resemblence between the two,' said Travis. The scotch was soaking pleasantly into his brain, deadening the painful memories of the day's events.

'Hey, making movies is my business, remember?'

'It *used* to be your business, Jack,' pointed out Travis, 'but that was when you were a . . . I use the term loosely . . . human being. Even your former colleagues might find it off-putting to do business with you in your present incarnation.'

'They'll never have to know. Most of my wheeling and dealing will continue to be done by phone and fax. But I'll need a front man at times and that's where you come in.'

'I don't know anything about making movies.'

'Good. That means there won't be any arguments between us. You'll simply do what I say.'

'That'll be the day.' Travis drank some more scotch.

'You'll thank me in the end. I'm gonna make us rich. Well, *semi*-rich.'

'Good,' said Beatrice. 'I'm tired of being poor.'

Travis looked at her. She was wearing a silver tiara, a silver

61

necklace and large silver bracelet. Sharon was similarly adorned with items from their Harrods heist. He sighed. 'I've got to get that stuff back to Harrods.'

'You're nuts,' Jack told him. 'We need it. We need to sell it.'

'You're the nutty one. I'm not risking prison. I had a taste of cell-life today and I don't want it to become a full-time occupation.'

'I told you, we need seed money to get this project rolling. We need to sell that stuff . . . unless you've got at least twenty thousand grand sitting in your bank account.'

'Hardly. I haven't even got two thousand. I had an expensive habit.'

'You and a drug habit? I find that hard to believe.'

'It wasn't a drug habit, it was Heather. But that's all in the past now.'

'Anyway, that settles it,' said Jack. 'We sell the crown jewels.'

Travis stared into his glass. 'I'm not saying yes, but, just out of curiosity, how would you go about doing that?'

'Easy. Find a fence.'

'But you've never been in London before. How would you find one?'

Jack winked at him. 'I know people who know people. Everywhere. Drop me in any city in the world and I'd soon find out who to deal with.'

'You're saying there's a worldwide brotherhood of cheap little crooks and you're a fully paid-up member?'

'Hey, watch your mouth, dickwit. I'm trying to help you out.'

'By having me become a dealer in stolen goods. Thank you very much. My gratitude knows no bounds.'

The phone rang. Jack flew over and picked it up. 'Arnie?' he barked. Then he looked annoyed and held out the phone to Travis. 'It's your dork of a boss.'

Travis took the phone. 'Hello Martin.'

'I see your unpleasant American friend is back in your flat again,' said Martin, disapprovingly.

' "Friend" is stretching it a bit, but yes, he is back. Look, I'm sorry about this afternoon.'

'So am I, Travis, so am I. I'm calling to give you one more chance. Have you come to your senses yet?'

'Well, that's a matter of opinion, Martin.'

'Are you now willing to tell me what's really going on with Prenderghast?'

'I wish I could. I really wish I could. But you wouldn't believe me. And I'm sorry about not delivering the story but as things stand it's no longer a possibility. All I can tell you is that I was right about Prederghast's virtual reality helmets presenting a danger to children. An even bigger danger than I suspected. You've got to print a warning!'

'I'd love to, if you'd only provide me with the evidence.'

'I can't. I'm sorry.'

'Then it's my turn to be sorry, Travis,' Martin told him crisply. 'I warned you. Your services are no longer required by *Watchdog* magazine. You're fired. You'll receive two months salary as per the terms of your contract. Don't bother coming into the office again. The contents of your desk will be forwarded to you. Goodbye, Travis.'

'Goodbye, Martin,' said Travis and hung up. He sighed and said to Jack, 'Okay, find your fence.'

David Whiteman was having supper with his wife Daphne in the sitting room of their house in Moor Park. Daphne was puzzled, and a little worried, because her husband had been unusually quiet during the meal. This wasn't like him because he liked – no, loved and adored – the sound of his own voice. She couldn't help giving a little jump of alarm when he suddenly said, 'Daphne, I have something serious to tell you.'

'You have?' she asked.

He looked her in the eye, his expression, like the tone of his voice, very serious indeed. 'Yes. Something happened to me today.'

'Oh, really? What?'

'I met a princess. From another planet. Her name was Beatrice. I also met a succubus. She came from the same planet. Her name was Sharon.'

Jesus Christ, thought Daphne.

'Both of them were very beautiful, Beatrice in particular. Just like a fairy princess, in fact, though I don't think she was a real fairy. But Sharon was definitely a succubus. She ate a piece of my soul. And she could turn invisible. Oh, and she could shrink in size as well.'

'Of course,' said Daphne, her mind racing. A terrible suspicion was beginning to form.

'This event has naturally changed my life. My rational world-view has been completely overturned,' he told her. 'I'm going to have to give up psychiatry. I have lost all faith in my former professional beliefs. I'm thinking of training for a new career – as an aromatherapist. What do you think, dear?'

She stared back at him for a time, then dropped her knife and fork on the table. 'You can't fool me!' she cried as she rose to her feet. 'All this rubbish is your way of telling me you've found out!'

He frowned. 'Found out what?'

'Oh, you can stop this silly act now! You somehow found out! You found out that I've been having an affair with your sister, Audrey, for the last two years!'

'You *what?!*' Suddenly all thoughts of fairy princesses, succubi and aromatherapy fled from David Whiteman's mind.

'All right, I'm willing to accept that with the money from the jewellery you'll be able to raise enough other finances, through your connections, to make a movie . . .'

'At last, I've got through to you,' applauded Jack.

'. . . But there are a few little details I'm still not clear on.'

'Shoot.'

'Don't tempt me. I've still got that Colt automatic, remember.'

'Stop jerking me around. What's still bothering you?'

'Well, for example, there's a thing called a screenplay. I may be a novice in this area but I do know a screenplay is a big help in the making of a movie.'

'Easy. You're going to write it.'

'*Me*? But I'm a journalist. Or I was . . .'

'You're a writer, aren't you? So you can write a screenplay.'

'But I've never written fiction before.'

Jack laughed unpleasantly. 'Show me a journalist who's never written fiction and I'll show you a bare-faced liar.'

Travis bristled. 'I resent that!'

'Resent it later. We're talking business here, dickwit. And I say you can write a screenplay. With help from me, natch.'

'And what is this screenplay going to be about? Or haven't you got to that bit yet?'

'Sure I have. It's going to be about you and your adventures.'

'My adventures? I haven't had any adventures!'

'Oh yeah? You've just returned from another world where you fought dragons, rescued princesses, outwitted an evil vampire prince and his sorcerer and became involved with cute and interesting demons. If they aren't adventures, what are they, dickwit?'

Travis thought this over. 'I thought of them as ordeals rather than as adventures,' he said at last.

'You think of me as an *ordeal*?' asked Beatrice, affronted.

'A beautiful ordeal, Beatrice, but an ordeal just the same,' Travis told her frankly.

'Humph,' she said.

'It's a perfect subject,' continued Jack enthusiastically. 'Fantasy movies are socko right now, according to Arnie. We've got a plot made to order and these two unworldly, knock-out babes to play themselves.' He indicated Beatrice and Sharon who both looked pleased, even if they weren't sure what he was talking about.

'But what if they can't act?' asked Travis.

'They won't need to. Believe me, the camera will have an orgasm over them.'

'And who is going to play you?'

'Me. I'm gonna play me.'

'You're going to reveal yourself?' asked Travis, surprised.

'Yeah. You're going to pass me off as a fiendishly clever special effect.'

'Oh. And I suppose I'm going to play me.'

'Nah,' said Jack, shaking his head. 'We're gonna need a real actor to play you. Someone who's also a good-looking hunk. And an American to boot. We need an American name – doesn't have to be too big but definitely a name – to appeal to the US market.'

'I'm going to be played by an American?' Travis asked slowly.

'You got to admit it makes sense,' said Jack. 'And don't take this the wrong way but you're not exactly moviestar material. I mean, you fill out a pair of tights okay and your face doesn't scare horses but, well . . . you get the picture.'

'Yes, I get the picture all right,' muttered Travis. Then he breathed out a long sigh. 'The picture I've got is that I'm not going to be in the picture.' He stood up and stretched. 'This is all too much for me right now. I'm exhausted. I'm going to bed. See you folks in the morning . . . Unfortunately.' He put the empty whisky glass on the table and began to head towards his bedroom.

'Ahem,' said Beatrice.

He stopped and looked at her. 'You "ahemmed",' he told her. He had a bad feeling that her 'ahem' augered problems for him.

'I did.'

'I know I'm going to regret this but why did you "ahem"?'

'You said you were going to bed,' said Beatrice.

'Yes. So why does that warrant an "ahem" heavy with significance?'

'There's only one bed,' pointed out Beatrice.

He nodded. 'Yes, that's true.'

'So where am I going to sleep?'

He frowned. 'I don't know,' he admitted. 'Same place as you slept last night? The living room couch, I presume.'

'I was too excited to sleep last night. Also you were in a bad way and obviously needed to be put to bed.'

'Good grief,' he muttered. 'Look, it's a double bed. Can't we simply share it? I promise you, I'll be good. I'm too tired to even think such thoughts . . .'

'Travis, you know why I can't share a bed with you,' she said primly.

He didn't, not at first, but then he remembered. 'Oh yes, because you're a princess and I'm a commoner.'

'Yes. You're very nice as commoners go, and I'm indebted to you for all sorts of reasons, but that doesn't alter the situation.'

Travis had an idea. 'I know! As a princess you can knight me! And as *Sir* Travis Thomson there'd be no reason why we couldn't share the bed. Hang on . . . you'll need a sword . . .' He went to the cutlery drawer and produced a bread knife. 'Will this do?'

She shook her head. 'It doesn't matter, Travis. I don't have the authority to knight you.'

'Bugger.' He threw the knife back in the drawer. 'So how come I lose the bed to you? Why don't you just sleep on the couch?'

She looked surprised. 'Why Travis, I'm a guest in your home. A *royal* guest. Of course you would offer me your bed.'

It was hopeless. He had run out of arguments. 'Okay, okay, I'll take the couch.' Then he looked wearily at Sharon. 'Unless you want it?'

'No. But I'd be happy to share the couch with you,' she told Travis.

'Thanks, but no thanks. I don't want to wake up and find myself short of one soul as a result of you deciding you wanted a snack in the middle of the night.'

'You know I wouldn't do that to you, Travis,' she said.

'Not intentionally, perhaps, but maybe you eat in your sleep. Besides, the couch isn't big enough for two.'

'What about me?' asked Jack.

'You can sleep in the fridge for all I care,' Travis told him.

'Some host you are, dickwit. No matter, I can hole up anywhere.' He leered at Sharon. 'How's this for an idea, gorgeous? You shrink yourself down to my size and we spend the night doing disgusting things to each other's bodies?'

'As ideas go, it's not going anywhere,' said Sharon. 'I've gone off you, Jack.'

'Rats . . .'

'You can share the bed with me, Sharon,' Beatrice told her.

'Thank you, Your Highness.'

Travis stared at Beatrice. 'Hey, hang on a minute! How come you'd let her sleep in the bed with you? Surely she's a commoner too!'

'Don't be silly, Travis,' said Beatrice, as if talking to someone incredibly dense. 'She's a succubus. Succubi can't be commoners, only humans can.'

'Oh.' Then he said, 'But what about your . . .' and stopped because he remembered that succubi only ate the souls of mortal *men*. Beatrice would be perfectly safe . . .

'Oh,' he said again, realizing as the thought of Beatrice and Sharon in the same bed together took an increasingly firm root in his mind that it would be impossible for him to get any sleep tonight.

Chapter Nine

Prince Valerie was reading a James Herbert novel and Damion was sitting at the dining table making one pound coins. Damion found it tedious work but so far hadn't mastered the intricacies of reproducing the paper money used in this world.

They were in the living quarters of the Tug and Pullet's landlord, a Mr Sydney Street. Mr Street and his family had graciously offered the place to Prince Valerie and Damion and had moved to alternative accommodation.

The Prince put the Herbert book down with a sigh of satisfaction. It was the second Herbert novel he'd read in a row. The landlord owned a complete set of Herbert's work. 'Damn fine writer, this Herbert fellow,' the Prince told Damion. 'I'd like to meet him someday.'

'I'm glad you're having fun,' muttered Damion as another pound coin materialised in a puff of sulphurous smoke. 'I'm working my magic to the bone here.'

'All in a good cause, Damion,' said the Prince. 'We have to keep our new subjects happy.'

'Happy? They're already bloody delirious, especially after we dealt with that rival gang a few blocks away.' The said rivals, based at a pub called the Rampant Cock, had undergone a radical change of heart since being visited by the Prince and Damion, and the Cock was now a community care centre offering homoeopathic treatments and counselling. The Rampant Cock had become an alcohol-free zone and its name had been changed to The Happy Hen.

'Still, I want them well supplied with money,' said the Prince. 'Another couple of hundred will do for now.'

'Bloody hell,' muttered Damion. 'There must be an easier way. And I don't see why we're wasting our time here when

69

we should be tracking down Travis and his damned companions.'

'They can wait. No hurry. I'm enjoying myself in this strange new world. And I can't remember the last time I had a vacation.'

'You've *never* had a vacation, sire,' said Damion. 'Vacations are unknown back in Samella.'

'Exactly my point,' said the Prince. 'I definitely needed one. Besides, what's waiting for me in Samella? Stroppy peasants and a legion of army widows demanding compensation for their missing husbands. And try getting a date when everyone knows you're a vampire. Hah!'

Damion looked around the room and wrinkled his nose. 'Don't tell me you're also enjoying these somewhat less than luxurious lodgings?'

'Ah, there you have a point,' nodded the Prince. 'Today we must find lodgings more suitable to my royal status. The question is where we can find such a thing . . . Summon Barry at once. He might know.'

Damion stopped his coin-making activities for a moment and clapped his hands. Seconds later the door opened and Barry Simmons entered. He bowed his head to the Prince and said, 'You wanted me, your Royal Guvnorship?'

'Yes, my doltish friend. We need to pick at what could laughingly be called your brains.'

Barry looked pleased. 'Sure, master. Pick away.'

'It's not that we're not grateful for the use of this humble – very humble – abode, but Damion and I would prefer more luxurious surroundings. Are there any available in this area?'

Barry frowned. 'You mean you want to move to somewhere posh, master?'

'I suppose so . . .'

'The Docklands would be your best bet, but a real fancy pad there would cost you a lot of dosh?'

'Is dosh like posh?' asked the Prince.

'Dosh . . . moolah . . . cash . . .' Barry pointed at the pile of pound coins on the table. 'That stuff.'

'Oh, I see. And how many of them would we require?'

'Hundreds of thousands of them, master,' Barry told him.

Another gold coin popped into existence and joined the pile. Damion groaned. 'Hundreds of *thousands*?' he complained. 'That would take me months!'

'There's easier ways to make money,' said Barry.

'Not as far as I know,' said Damion, bitterly.

'Why don't you just knock over a bank?'

The Prince looked at Barry. 'What is a bank?' he asked.

'I don't know where to begin,' Travis told Jack as he stared at the screen of his Apple Macintosh.

'Just knock out a rough outline, describing what happened to you on Samella,' Jack advised him. 'Once we get the structure right we can flesh it out.'

'You make it sound so bloody easy,' muttered Travis. 'But where do I start?'

'Coming up with a title first is always a good idea,' said Jack.

Travis tried to think of a title – something that would sum up his experiences on Samella – but his mind remained as blank as his computer screen.

Jack made a suggestion. 'How about *Planet of the Babes*?'

Travis groaned.

'Yeah, you're right,' said Jack, lighting up the inevitable Marlboro. 'A bit too crude.' He was perched on the printer next to the word processor. Travis waved irritably at the smoke. 'By the way, I've fixed you up for a meeting with a fence. It's on for this afternoon.'

'What?' yelped Travis.

'Half past three at a bar in the east side of the city, called Walford or something,' Jack continued. 'And the bar is called the Tug and Pullet.'

'You want me to meet a fence? And in Walford? Bloody hell, even the police don't go there without an SAS escort!'

'Don't be a wimp. All you do is meet this guy in the bar,

hand the stuff over to him and he'll hand you an envelope full of cash. No problems.'

'Not for you, maybe, but plenty for me,' said Travis. 'I'll be taking all the risks. How can you trust this . . . this fence?'

'Hey, he's been vouched for by people I trust,' Jack told him. 'Well, maybe *trust* is putting it a bit too strongly but as crooks go they're okay.'

'Well, now I feel completely confident. How do you know this isn't a police set-up?'

'Nah, no chance.'

'How will I recognise this character?'

'You won't. He'll recognise you. He's been supplied a full description of you.'

'This gets worse and worse.'

'Look, we need the money. Just do it.'

Travis knew only too well that they did need the money. Earlier that morning he had driven Beatrice and Sharon down to Selfridges and had them outfitted with clothes and various accessories, an act which had practically depleted his bank account. He sighed. 'I guess I'll do it.'

The doorbell rang. Travis automatically jumped with alarm. He never used to do that when the bell rang but now it had become a habit. 'Stay here,' he told Jack as he rose from his chair. He went into the sitting room and saw that Beatrice and Sharon, wearing two of their new outfits, were watching TV. On the screen Travis glimpsed a man leaping wildly back and forth across a large, floating map of Britain. 'Behave yourselves,' he warned them as he passed by.

He opened the front door. It was Stephen, wearing his usual wide grin. 'Hi!' he said.

'What do you want?' asked Travis curtly.

'Travis, you've really got to work on those social skills of yours. Your standards are slipping . . .' said Stephen as he pushed by Travis. 'I've come to take one of your lovely cousins to lunch. Where are they?'

Travis helplessly followed Stephen first into the kitchen

and then the living room. 'Hi Sharon . . . Beatrice,' greeted Stephen.

Beatrice gave him a polite smile while Sharon beamed lasciviously at him. Travis had never seen a lascivious beam before. 'Hello Stephen,' breathed Sharon as she rose to her feet. 'Do you like my new clothes?' She rotated in front of him. She was wearing a black leather miniskirt and a low cut, blood-red blouse. They had been her choice, not Travis's. She had even chosen the black leather boots. Travis hoped she was also wearing one of the pairs of knickers he'd insisted buying for her but wouldn't want to bet on it.

'You look wonderful,' said Stephen, obviously meaning it. 'I was just telling Travis that I've come to take you out to lunch.'

'Oh, that's great,' she said.

Stephen looked at Travis and said, 'Unless your *cousin* here has an objection?'

Travis had tried to warn Stephen about Sharon and he could see that it would be useless to try again. He gave a shrug.

'Good,' said Stephen, turning back to Sharon. 'There's a marvellous little Italian place not far from here. Do you like Italian?'

'Sure,' said Sharon brightly, then, 'What is it?'

'Food. Italian food,' said Stephen, a little taken aback. 'Do you like Italian food?'

'Oh yes, I *love* Italian food!' she exclaimed, taking him by the arm. 'Let's go!'

But Stephen hesitated and said to Beatrice, not very convincingly, 'Would you like to come too, Beatrice?'

'No thanks,' she told him, clearly having sized up the situation. 'I'll stick with Richard and Judy.'

'Who the hell are they?' cried Travis, looking wildly around. *Don't tell me I've got more uninvited guests*, he thought.

'That's them,' said Beatrice, pointing at the screen. Travis saw a man and woman, both with blonde hair, sitting in front

73

of a glass wall and grinning, a mite frantically it seemed to him, into the camera.

'Oh,' he said, relieved.

When Stephen and Sharon had gone, Travis returned to his study and sat down at the processor. Jack asked him who it had been at the door. Travis told him, and about Stephen taking Sharon out to lunch.

'Whooo-boy,' laughed Jack. 'Does he have any idea what he's biting off?'

'I'm more concerned about what Sharon is going to bite off,' he said as he began typing. 'But I think I've got a title . . .'

Jack peered round at the screen. '*Damned and Fancy*?' he read aloud. 'It's snappy, I guess, but what's it mean?'

'I haven't a clue,' said Travis, truthfully.

Travis locked the car and looked around nervously, trying to spot potential car thieves. Unfortunately everyone in the square looked like a potential car thief.

'You really look jumpy,' Beatrice told him.

'I told you, this is a dangerous area. I wish you hadn't insisted on coming.'

'I was bored. When *A Country Practice* was over there wasn't anything else interesting on TV. You really should think about getting a dish.'

Good grief, thought Travis, *And this was only her second day in this world* . . . 'There's the Tug and Pullet,' he said, pointing at the seedy exterior of a pub across the square. 'Come on, let's get this over with.'

'Are we going to have an adventure, Travis?'

'I sincerely hope not,' he sighed.

Bank teller Valerie Dickson would say later that she thought there was something suspicious about the two men as soon as they entered the bank. One was tall and carrying a canvas holdall bag, the other was shorter, younger, and walking with the aid of a stick. She thought there was something odd about their clothing: both wore ill-fitting suits and both had very long hair tied back in ponytails. Also, she later remembered that they both appeared unnaturally pale. They approached her window together. The taller one smiled at her and said, 'Good afternoon. Please read this.' And then he shoved a piece of paper under her security screen.

She read the note. It consisted of one sentence. She read it twice. It still didn't make sense. It said: 'Hand over all your available cash or we'll turn your colleague sitting on your right into a toad.'

She looked at the two men in turn. 'What do you mean . . . a toad?' she asked, wondering whether or not to push the silent alarm button right away. It might turn out to be just some kind of joke.

'I mean, a toad,' said the taller man impatiently. 'A largish amphibian closely related to the frog family. Surely you're familiar with toads. Now hand over the cash.'

'Are you armed?' she said nervously.

'Armed?' he asked haughtily. 'Where would I hide my rapier in these ridiculous clothes?'

From toads to talk of rape. Definitely time to hit the panic button, Valerie decided. So she pressed it. At the same time she tried to rise from her seat in order to throw herself flat on the floor in case they started shooting but found she was somehow stuck to the chair.

'The money,' said the tall man. 'Now!'

She froze. All she had to do was wait for the police to arrive. The reason why she was unable to get out of her chair could wait until later.

'I warned you,' said the man. 'Damion, do your stuff.'

She saw the small man waggle his fingers in the direction of her colleague, Peter Ferris, who so far was oblivious to what was happening. Peter immediately vanished and in his place was a large green toad.

'GROAK?' said the toad.

'I'm terribly sorry, Peter,' she told the toad. Finally her cash drawer was empty. 'That's all,' she told the tall man.

'Give me the toad's money as well,' he ordered.

Still unable to rise from her chair, she had to wheel it over to Peter's cash drawer. The tall man moved over to Peter's window. By now the other two tellers had become aware that something was wrong. One of them, Elrica Patel, said anxiously, 'What's happening?'

'The bank is being robbed by these two gentlemen,' Valerie told her. 'They're turned Peter into a toad so I have no choice but to do what they want.'

'Oh, right,' said Elrica, who couldn't think of anything else to say just then.

To Valerie's relief she heard the welcome sound of distant, but approaching, police sirens. She expected the two men to flee but to her surprise the sirens seemed to have no significance to them. But then a third man burst into the bank and yelled, 'Your Guvnorship! The filth are coming! We gotta go now or they'll catch us!'

'If you insist,' said the tall man with a sigh. He stopped shovelling money into his bag and headed towards the door. 'Come on, Damion.' But the short one paused to waggle his fingers again. The toad abruptly vanished and Peter was back in his chair. The short man then followed the other two out the door.

Peter slumped dizzily forward and clutched at his computer monitor. 'Wha' happened?' he moaned. Valerie, who discovered she was no longer stuck to the chair, got up and patted him on the shoulder.

'It's all right,' she told him. 'You got turned into a toad by a couple of bank robbers but you're okay now.'

'Get in, master! Quick!' urged Barry, who was already in the car. Nigel was behind the wheel. The sound of the sirens was getting louder.

Prince Valerie handed him the bag of money. 'Leave now. We'll make our own way back,' he told Barry.

76

'But . . .'

'GO!' thundered the Prince. The car sped off. The Prince and Damion then ducked into an alley beside a nearby Wimpy bar. There the Prince turned into a large night screet and Damion turned into a vactor. They both soared into the sky and began to fly off towards the Tug and Pullet.

Chapter Ten

When Travis and Beatrice entered the Tug and Pullet the place fell silent, like a bar in a western movie when the Stranger arrives. He put the blame on Beatrice – he'd tried dressing her down by making her wear a drab raincoat, a scarf around her head and dark glasses, but her ethereal beauty and sheer other-worldliness still shone through. Feigning indifference, he led her to the bar. A small woman with a large bosom and bright blonde hair, greeted them cheerfully. ' 'Allo, dears! What's your poison?'

Travis ordered drinks for them both and then cast furtive glances around the bar, trying to spot a likely-looking fence. Unfortunately, all the patrons of the Tug and Pullet – male and female – appeared to be suitable candidates. He noticed, with a shudder, a large portrait of the Krays on one of the walls.

Beatrice sipped her sweet sherry, wrinkled her nose and said, 'There's something wrong here.'

'I'm sorry. I'll order you something else.'

'It's just not the drink, it's this place. It doesn't feel right.'

'I'm not surprised. It's full of villains,' he whispered in her ear.

'It's not just the people here either,' she said firmly. 'I can sense something else. A presence. And it has the smell of Samella about it.'

'Really?' he said, taken aback. 'But how can that be?'

'I don't know,' she confessed.

Just then it was his turn to sense a presence. Or rather, to smell a bad case of B.O. He turned and saw that a fat man of about forty had sidled up to him. 'Travis?' asked the man quietly.

Travis nodded. 'And you're the fence?'

The man snarled. 'Don't call me that, you berk!'

'Sorry. I'm new at this. But I've got the stuff . . .' He rattled the Harrods bag. 'You have the money?'

'Careful!' muttered the man, glancing around warily. 'Not in here! That little guy just along the bar with the harelip is Edwards' snout.'

Travis looked at the little man with the harelip. 'What's a snout? And who's Edwards?'

The fence shook his head despairingly. 'Blimey, don't you watch *The Bill*? Edwards is D.I. Edwards. Detective Inspector Ramsey Edwards. This is his manor. And a snout is a grass. A snitch. An informer. Got the picture?'

'Only too well.'

'So we got to be careful. And there's something else that's worrying me . . .' The fence glanced around again. 'There's something not right here today.'

'How can you possibly tell?' Travis asked.

'I got a feeling in my water,' said the fence. 'Something's *changed* here. I'm picking up a funny atmosphere . . .'

'See, Travis?' said Beatrice. 'I told you the same thing.'

Travis looked around the pub. Apart from a lot of people he wouldn't want to meet in a dark alley – or even a bright alley – he couldn't see anything out of the ordinary.

'It's their eyes,' said the fence. 'They got a kind of glazed look, as if they're all on drugs or something.'

Travis looked more closely. He then saw what the fence meant. He was reminded of the time he had, while on an assignment for the magazine, infiltrated a meeting of Scientologists.

'We'll do it this way,' the fence told him. 'I'll go to the Gents and you wait a bit and then follow me. We'll do the switch in there.'

'Right,' said Travis. He was feeling even more nervous now, thanks to both Beatrice's and the fence's ominous warnings. He watched the fence move off towards the entrance to the toilet, then said to Beatrice, 'If I don't come back in a few minutes get the hell out of here.'

'Why would you not come back?' she asked.

'All sorts of bad reasons. Just do as I say.' He headed towards the Gents, feeling proud of his cool dialogue and ignoring a liquid sensation in his bowels.

Inside, the fence fidgeted nervously. 'Hurry up!' he urged.

Travis looked around. He had seen better, and cleaner, toilet facilities on Samella. He handed his bag to the fence who peered inside and quickly checked the merchandise. He finally nodded with satisfaction then produced a large brown envelope from inside his coat. Travis took it. 'Thanks . . .'

'Better count it,' said the fence.

'It's okay. I trust you.'

'Don't be a complete berk. Count it! And fast!'

Travis counted it. The envelope contained thirty thousand pounds in used tens and twenties, just as Jack said it would. He nodded. 'Yep, all here.'

'I'm off then,' said the fence. 'And you and your girl should get out of here quick smart too.' The fence left. Travis, realising he had an urgent need to relieve himself, used the urinal before following suit.

Beatrice, he was happy to see, was exactly where he'd left her. There was no sign of the fence. 'Come on, let's go,' he told her.

'Good,' she said as they hurried towards the front door. 'That bad feeling I have is getting worse . . .'

As they went out the door two young men brushed by them. The two young men were Barry and Nigel Simmons. And at that precise moment Prince Valerie and Damion, still in their respective screet and vactor forms, were landing on the roof of the Tug and Pullet.

'Hurry! Hurry!' urged Beatrice and broke into a trot. Travis followed, uncomfortably conscious of the envelope containing thirty thousand pounds pressed against his chest.

Prince Valerie and Damion turned back to their usual forms. Damion immediately began to sniff the air, his nose twitching violently.

'Damion, what's wrong with your nose?' Prince Valerie asked him.

'I can smell something . . .'

'You surprise me. Now if you *heard* something with your nose I'd be really impressed.'

'No, no, sire!' said Damion eagerly. 'I can smell Samella!'

'Poor you.'

'I left a guardian spell over the building, on the off-chance that any of our enemies made a visit during our absence. And they have. Two of them. They've just left, so they must still be close by.'

'Really?' said the Prince and smiled, showing his fangs. 'Show me where . . .'

Travis and Beatrice reached the car and quickly got in. 'Hurry! Hurry!' cried Beatrice.

'I am! I am!' he said as he started the engine. He pulled away from the kerb, and, picking up speed, drove out of the square.

'Damn!' said Damion, leaning over the edge of the roof. 'Nothing! They've left the area.'

'How disappointing,' said the Prince. 'Any idea who it was?'

'Only that it was a man and a woman,' said Damion, scanning the square.

'Not your succubus then?'

'No, definitely not that little bitch. I would have smelt her presence clearly.'

'In which case it had to be Travis and my dear, ex-fiancée Beatrice . . .'

'I wonder what they were up to . . .' said Damion.

'I think we should down to the bar and make enquiries,' said the Prince.

Detective Inspector Ramsey Edwards entered the bank and

was met by WPC Janet Weller. 'What have we got here, Janet?' he asked her briskly.

'Well,' she began hesitantly, 'It's all kind of odd, sir. There appears to have been a robbery but the main witnesses are telling stories that are downright strange.'

'Strange?' asked DI Edwards as he stared balefully around the bank and then at the assembled witnesses. 'Strange in what way?'

'Sir . . . stories about a male teller being turned into a toad . . . sir.'

'*What*?! Sounds like someone has been pulling your chain, Janet,' he thundered. 'I want the facts, not fairy stories!'

'I'm sorry, sir,' said WPC Weller, quaking, 'but that's what they're saying.' She consulted her notepad. 'A witness, Miss Valerie Dickson, who was one of the two tellers he robbed, gave the following account: ''I was approached by two unusual-looking men, one of whom passed me a note demanding all my cash otherwise my colleague, Peter Ferris, would be turned into a toad. I refused and, to my surprise, Peter *was* turned into a toad . . .'' '

DI Edwards held up his hand. 'Enough!' He looked around. 'Where is this looney tune?'

'Over there,' said the WPC, indicating a young, chubby woman, who was standing with an asian woman and a young man with an ashen face. DI Edwards strode over to the little group and glared down at Valerie Dickson. 'What is all this bloody rubbish about people turning into toads?!' he demanded angrily.

She gave him an indignant look. 'It's not rubbish. That's what happened. Peter here got turned into a toad.'

'It's true,' chipped in the asian woman. 'Peter became a great big frog.'

'*Something* weird definitely happened to me,' said the young man, shakily. 'One minute I was sitting there feeling my normal self and the next I couldn't see over the counter. And all I could say was ''*GRURK*!''.'

'Actually, it was more like ''GROAK!'',' said Valerie,

82

helpfully. DI Edwards stared hard at them each in turn. Finally he boomed, 'It's a conspiracy! You're all in this together! You've dreamed up this ridiculous story to cover up your own involvement in the robbery!'

'Excuse me,' said a smartly-dressed middle-aged man as he stepped forward. 'But you have no right to accuse these three of any wrong-doing . . .'

DI Edwards turned on the man. 'And who might you be?'

'I'm Roger Preston, the assistant manager, and I can vouch for the characters of all three of these employees, especially for Miss Dickson who has been with the bank since she left school.'

'That's not good enough,' snarled DI Edwards. 'For all I know, you could be part of it too.'

A little old lady holding a crash helmet also stepped forward. 'They're telling the truth,' she told DI Edwards. 'That young man *did* turn into a toad. I saw it. And if you call me a liar I'll kick you in the goolies.'

DI Edwards took a quick step back. 'This is the most unbelievable nonsense I'll ever hear in this job.'

He was wrong because just then Detective Sergeant Dick Spencer entered the bank with a shabbily dressed man in his late fifties. 'Guv, this character saw the getaway. Even got the number of the car, or so he said.'

'What do you mean?' asked DI Edwards.

'Well, I radioed the number into the control room just now and they called me back to say there's no such car registration on record.'

DI Edwards leaned close to the shabby man. He could smell alcohol on his breath. 'You've been drinking,' he accused him.

'You bet I have,' said the man. 'If you saw what I saw today you'd have hit the bottle as well.'

'And what exactly did you see?'

'I saw three blokes come rushing out of the bank. One of them got in the car, a red Ford Escort, and drove off with another bloke. The other two went into the alley next to the Wimpy bar.'

'Did they?' asked DI Edwards, surprised. 'But that's a dead end.'

'Yeah, I know. So I popped my head round the corner to have a quick gander . . .' He stopped and shook his head in wonderment.

'And?' prompted DI Edwards.

'I saw something bloody incredible. That's why I needed to go and get a stiff drink.'

'So what did you bloody well see?!' demanded DI Edwards.

'These two blokes . . . they changed . . .'

'They changed their clothing?'

'No, no! They *changed!* Into some sort of creatures! Bloody great big things they were, kind of like giant bats but they had different heads. Really scary heads! And they weren't solid, either. You could kind of see through them . . .'

'You could see through them, eh?' said DI Edwards in a flat voice.

'Yeah, yeah! They were all hazy . . .'

'Hazy? Right. Then what happened?'

'They took off. Just flapped their wings and flew away.'

'Flew away,' repeated DI Edwards. Right then he wished he could fly away. 'Like little birdies?'

'Like bloody big birdies, Constable.'

That was it for DI Edwards. 'Right, you're nicked!' He turned and pointed at Valerie Dickson and the other witnesses. 'You're all nicked! For wasting police time! And you're going to stay nicked until I get to the bottom of this load of bloody bollocks!'

'. . . and she was a real looker, like a movie star,' continued the landlord's wife, Babs. 'She stood out a mile among this miserable mob.'

'And the man with her? What did he look like?' the Prince asked.

84

Babs shrugged. 'Ordinary looking geezer. About thirty. Spoke proper so he wasn't from around here. But nothing about him that would make you look twice. I remember thinking at the time that a girl like her would be way out of his league and I wondered why she was with him.'

'That's Travis all right,' said Damion.

'Yes . . .' said the Prince, stroking his chin. 'The question is, what he and Beatrice were doing here.'

'Looking for us, of course.'

'I don't like the implications of this development,' said the Prince thoughtfully. 'Perhaps Travis has powers in this world that we are, as yet, unaware of.'

'You seriously think he might pose a threat to us?'

'Sounds unlikely I know, but look how he managed to bugger up both our lives back in our own world. We must be cautious.'

'I suppose so,' said Damion doubtfully.

'And in the meantime,' added the Prince, 'the sooner we establish a new base, the better.' He took the holdall bag from Barry and opened it. He dumped its contents on the bar. 'Will this be enough for our new home?'

'Nah,' said Barry. 'Not nearly enough. I reckon we'll have to knock over at least another couple of banks before you've got the necessary funds.'

The Prince rolled his eyes. 'Right, then, let's get moving.'

Travis tossed the envelope down on the table. 'There's your dirty money,' he told Jack.

'*Our* dirty money, you mean,' said Jack, as he flew over and eagerly opened the envelope. 'It's gonna save our bacon.'

'Keep telling me that and one day I may believe you,' sighed Travis as he poured himself a drink.

'Any problems?' asked Jack.

'Not really. Beatrice had a serious attack of bad vibes in that pub. Funnily enough, so did the fence. But nothing happened.' He took a swallow of scotch and soda. 'What time did Sharon get back?'

'She didn't. She's still out with your dorky best buddy.'

Scotch and soda went up the back of Travis's nose. 'She's what?!' he gasped.

'I said, she hasn't come back yet.'

Travis slammed down his glass and raced for the front door, hoping he wouldn't be too late.

Chapter Eleven

'So you insist on sticking to your ridiculous story?' DI Edwards asked the tramp, whose name was Bernard Davenport.

'I have to. It's the only ridiculous story I've got.'

DI Edwards swore under his breath. Earlier he had been swearing aloud until WPC Janet Weller reminded him that his obscenities would be picked up on the interview room's tape recorder. He took a deep breath and tried to stay calm. 'Look you admit you're an alcoholic. Surely you must agree that it's more likely that what you *thought* you saw was an alcoholic hallucination?'

'I'm not an alcoholic,' protested Bernard. 'I'm a heavy social drinker.'

'Social drinker?' scoffed DI Edwards. 'You live in the street with all the other drunken no-hopers!'

'Can't get more social than that.'

DI Edwards took another deep breath. 'You were wrong about the car's number,' he pointed out.

'No, I wasn't. I'm very good with numbers. I used to be a tax inspector.'

'But there's no record of any car with that registration number!' cried DI Edwards.

Bernard shrugged. 'Can't help that. I know what I saw. That was the number on the getaway car.'

'That's not possible.'

Bernard smiled slyly at DI Edwards. 'I reckon if those blokes can turn themselves into giant bat-thingies and fly away, then fixing a mere number plate would be child's play for them. Don't you?'

'You're not going to give up on that, are you?'

'Does the fat lady sing in the woods?'

DI Edwards brought his fist down on the table top in irritation. 'All right. I don't know what motive you've got to concoct this pile of rubbish but I've had enough of you. You're free to go. Get out of my sight.'

Bernard stood up. 'Thank you, Constable. Only trying to help.'

'Get out.'

Bernard hesitated then held out his hand. 'Er, you couldn't spare some change, could you, Constable?'

'*MOVE IT!*' thundered DI Edwards.

Bernard left.

DI Edwards groaned and rubbed his eyes. 'Give me strength,' he said.

'What now, sir?' asked WPC Janet Weller.

'Well, while we wait for the SOCO team to produce some results I suppose I'd better talk to that woman teller again, Dickson. Go fetch her, please.'

Valerie Dickson was not looking very happy when she was escorted back into the interview room. 'I want a lawyer,' she told him sternly.

He forced out a smile which he hoped mingled reassurance with paternal concern. 'Miss Dickson, I just want to ask you some more questions. You're not being charged with anything.'

'That's not what you said before.'

He tried to look contrite. 'I was upset. Said things I shouldn't have. I apologise.'

'I should think so,' said Valerie. 'You were incredibly rude, even for a policeman.'

DI Edwards just managed to keep the smile in place. 'As I said, I'm sorry. Now can we go over your recollection of what happened at the bank one more time. Please.'

'Why? You're not going to believe me.'

'Miss Dickson, I'll be honest with you – I can't believe what you say happened did happen, but I do now believe that you believe what you saw.'

'You're saying you think I'm crazy?'

'No, no,' he said hastily. 'I'm saying that you and the other witnesses were somehow *influenced* into seeing what you thought you saw. By hypnosis, maybe.'

She thought about it. 'This happens a lot, does it?' she asked him, tartly. 'Bank robbers hypnotise tellers into thinking their workmates have been turned into toads? I've never seen it shown on *Crimewatch*.'

'It's not a common event, no,' Edwards growled. 'In fact, it's a first in my experience. But it's the only rational explanation. You must agree about that.'

She shrugged. 'I only know what I saw.'

At that moment there was a knock on the door and a constable entered. 'Sorry to interrupt, sir,' he told the DI, 'but I've got SOCO's preliminary report . . .'

'Good,' said the DI, eagerly, snatching the paper from the constable's hand. 'Now at last we'll get some hard facts . . .' But as he read the report he started to frown. 'I don't understand this,' he said.

'What does it say, sir?' asked WPC Weller.

'SOCO tested the note given to Miss Dickson here by the robbers,' he said slowly. 'They found prints all right, including those belonging to Miss Dickson. The problem is that the other prints are blank.'

'Blank, sir?' asked WPC Weller, blankly.

'The other prints have no prints. Whoever handled the notes apart from Miss Dickson had completely smooth fingers.' He screwed up the paper and tossed it in a bin. 'That's a lot of help, I don't think.'

The phone rang. WPC Weller answered it and listened. Then she said, 'Yes, I'll tell him.' She put the phone down. 'That was the control room, sir. There's been another bank robbery. In Crowley Road. Officers at the scene report unusual circumstances . . .'

'Like what?' snapped DI Edwards.

'Er . . . witnesses at the bank claim they saw a bank teller turned into a small, furry animal. Possibly a possum but there's some disagreement among the witnesses about that.'

89

'A possum?'

'That's what they said, sir. Sorry.'

'Can I go home now?' Valerie Dickson asked him, and gave him a sweet smile.

He stared at her, then sighed and said, 'Yes, of course. Go.'

Valerie rose from her chair. After a pause, said, 'There's something I suppose I should tell you.'

'If it involves toads or small, furry animals, I don't want to hear it,' he said, grimly.

'It's about the third man. The one who came running into the bank to warn the other two that the filth were coming.'

'What about him?'

'I recognised him. His name is Barry Simmons. My older sister, Jackie, used to go out with him for a while but she got better.'

He gaped at her. 'You knew the man? Why the hell didn't you tell me this before?!' he demanded.

'Because you were so rude to me,' Valerie told him, smiling sweetly once more.

Travis leant on Stephen's doorbell. Finally he heard sounds of movement in the flat. The door opened. Stephen, wearing a dressing gown, peered out. To Travis he looked completely shagged out. Travis wasn't sure whether that was because Sharon had been munching on his soul or because he was simply completely shagged out.

'Oh, it's you, Travis . . . what's up?'

'I was worried about you,' Travis told him. 'I presume Sharon is still with you.'

'And how,' Stephen said, and gave him a wink and a bleary, satisfied grin.

'Do you feel all right?' Travis asked him anxiously.

'Never better, mate. Though I've used muscles today I never knew I had. I'll probably ache like buggery tomorrow, but it's been worth it.'

Sharon appeared beside Stephen. She was, of course,

naked. Her expression was that of a contented cat. 'Hello, Travis,' she said. 'What's the problem.'

'You are. Come on. We're going home.'

'No, I'm not. I'm having fun.'

'I'll bet you are. Go on, get your things. You're leaving.'

Sharon stuck her tongue out at him. Stephen put a proprietorial arm around her shoulders. 'You can't force her, Travis. She's a big girl. She can make her own decisions. Can't you, darling?' Sharon nodded and licked his ear.

'Stephen, you don't understand,' said Travis desperately. 'You're in danger!'

'Well, yeah, she does have pretty sharp teeth but she's promised to be more careful in future.'

'It's not just her teeth . . .'

'Relax, Travis,' said Sharon. 'I've only had the smallest of nibbles . . .'

'You call that a small nibble?' asked Stephen. 'I almost went through the ceiling.' He laughed and gave her an affectionate squeeze.

'We're not talking about . . . *that* sort of thing,' said Travis.

'Then what are you talking about?'

Travis looked at Sharon. She winked at him. He threw up his hands in surrender. 'All right, have it your way. I give up. Do whatever you want. Just don't say I didn't warn you, Stephen.'

'I won't. Whatever it is you're trying to warn me about. You're really acting strange lately, Travis. You never used to be a killjoy.'

'There are a lot of things I never used to be,' said Travis wearily. 'Maybe one day I'll tell you the full story. In the meantime, just be careful of her . . . teeth.'

'I will. Bye Travis.'

'Yes, bye Travis,' said Sharon, grinning at him.

Stephen closed the door. Travis heard laughter from inside. He turned and headed down the corridor, unsure of what to do next. He didn't fancy returning to his flat right away. Jack would start hounding him to work on the wretched screen-play. But where else could he go. . . ?

Tod the barman wasn't pleased to see him. 'Haven't you been barred?' he asked as Travis sat on a bar stool.

'Not to my knowledge. According to the rules it would take a committee meeting to have my membership cancelled, and somehow I don't think there's been a committee meeting since I was last here. I'll have a double scotch and soda.'

Tod regarded him doubtfully. 'I'll have to check with the manager,' he said and reached for the phone.

'Go ahead,' Travis told him. 'And give Chris my regards.' He looked around the bar. There were only three other members present. A young couple sitting at a table and the inevitable Harry Adam Knight perched on his usual stool at the end of the bar.

After a brief conversation Tod hung up and said to Travis, 'Chris said I have to serve you but not any of your friends.'

'Do you see any of my friends in the vicinity?'

'No,' admitted Tod.

'Then I'll have that double scotch and soda.'

As he was being served Travis saw Harry Adam Knight get off his stool and head in his direction, staggering a little as he walked. 'G'day, mate,' said Knight, in a strong Australian accent, thrusting out a hand. 'Harry Adam Knight's the name, hack-writing is the game . . .'

Travis should his hand. 'Yes, I know who you are, Mr Knight. I'm Travis Thomson.'

Knight managed to climb onto the next barstool. 'Call me Harry, mate.' He was a thin man in his late forties and dressed in a crumpled dark blue suit. Travis thought he resembled a younger William Burroughs. But then *everyone* was younger than William Burroughs. He wasn't sure whether or not he welcomed this sudden display of sociability from the horror writer who had always ignored him up until now. Travis took a large swallow of scotch and soda and lit a cigarette. 'I'll have to come clean right away and admit that I haven't read any of your novels.'

Knight lit a cigarette of his own, coughed and laughed at the same time and said, 'You and the rest of the population, mate. Truth is I'm a bit of a sticky-beak and after seeing your spot of strife in here yesterday with the three young cracking sheilas and the other bloke I couldn't help wondering what it was all about. And today you come in looking lower than a snake's wedding tackle so I thought I'd come right out and ask you straight. But if you don't want to talk just tell me to bugger off out of it. I can take a hint, mate.'

Travis debated with himself how to respond, then decided what the hell and proceeded to give Knight an abridged description of what had been happening to him lately. Pausing only when they had to order rounds of drinks at regular intervals, Travis talked for over an hour. When he finished Knight nodded sympathetically and said, 'I know how you feel, mate. I've been in similar situations myself.'

'You have?' asked Travis, surprised.

'Yeah, sure I have.' Then he added, 'Of course they didn't involve demons, fairy princesses, vampires, sorcerers, other worlds and all that stuff but otherwise . . . yeah, I've been there all right.'

'Oh,' said Travis and ordered another round of drinks.

Detective Inspector Edwards listened as the debate continued among the witnesses as to whether the bank teller, one Yvonne Campbell, had been turned into a possum or some other species of small mammal. The warning note passed to the other teller was no help; it simply said 'Hand over all your cash or we'll turn the colleague sitting on your left into a small, furry animal.' The description of the two robbers matched that given by the witnesses in the other bank which was the only thing that made any sense. DI Edwards felt like going home, getting into bed and pulling the duvet up over his head until all this madness went away.

Detective Sergeant Dick Spencer, who had been talking on

his radio, came over and said, 'Some good news, guv. They've picked up Barry Simmons. He was at the Tug and Pullet, just like you said he'd be.'

'Great!' cried the DI, rubbing his hands. 'You stay here and finish getting their looney statements. I'm heading back to the nick. Maybe now we'll get to the bottom of this crazy business!'

When DI Edwards arrived back at the station the police van was just pulling up in the car park. He parked his car beside it and eagerly jumped out. Uniforms were climbing out of the back of the van. He couldn't see Simmons. 'Where is he?' he demanded as he pushed past them and peered into the van. Simmons wasn't there. He turned on the group of uniformed officers. 'You said you had him! Where the hell is he?'

One of the uniforms, a Constable John Parker, said, in a puzzled voice, 'He's right here, sir.' And he pointed to his side. Then DI Edwards noticed that a pair of handcuffs hung from Parker's wrist.

Slowly, DI Edwards said to Constable Parker, 'He's right here is he? You've got him cuffed, have you?'

Looking even more puzzled, Constable Parker nodded and said, 'Sure, he's right here!'

On impulse, DI Edwards suddenly clapped his hands very loudly in front of Parker's face. The young constable reacted with surprise, then blinked and looked around and then down at the empty cuffs dangling from his wrist. Then in a tone of amazement he said, 'Bloody hell! He's gone!'

Chapter Twelve

'I wasn't always a writer, you know. I had loads of jobs back in Australia,' said Harry Adam Knight in a slurred voice. 'I was a cook, truck driver, barman, undertaker's assistant, pearl diver, brickie, gold miner and a door-to-door lingerie salesman.' He took another drink. 'Busiest bloody week of my life, that was.'

'Why did you leave Australia, Harry?' asked Travis in an equally slurred voice.

'Ah, that's a sore point, mate. Lot of bitter memories tied up with that. It was a sheila, of course.'

'A woman?'

'Yeah, it's always a woman at the root of it. Always.'

'Yeah,' agreed Travis, then after some thought added, 'Unless it's a man.'

'Pardon me?'

'I said, unless it's a man. If you were gay it would be a man at the root of it.'

'Oh . . . yeah,' said Knight and gave him a wary look. 'You a shirt-lifter, are you? Not that I have anything against you perverts. Some of my best friends are perverts.'

'No, no, I'm not gay, I was just pointing out that if you *were* gay it would be a man at the root of it all.'

'Ah, right,' said Knight and took another drink.

'So you were really in love with this woman, were you?'

'What woman?'

'The woman who made you leave Australia.'

'Oh, that one. Yeah, I loved her all right. I loved her so much I would have crawled on my hands and knees all the way across the Nullabor Plain just to hear her piss in an empty kerosene can.'

'Sounds serious,' said Travis, impressed.

'Too right it was serious, mate.'

'So what happened? She leave you for another man?'

'Nah. She left me for other *men*.'

'Other men?'

'Yeah. The local cricket team. The Burrandini First Eleven to be exact. She would have shagged the Second Eleven as well if there had been one.'

'Er, I see,' said Travis, uncomfortably. 'A tad over-sexed, was she?'

'Over-sexed? The only time she put her thighs together was to open a bottle of wine.'

'I see,' Travis said again, though this time he didn't.

'And the dirty little mole had the nerve to blame me! Said I couldn't satisfy her between the sheets!'

Travis nodded. 'No man likes to be accused by his woman of being sexually inadequate.'

'Nah. Especially if she takes out an ad about it in the local rag. Which is what she did. The ratbag.'

'So that's why you left Australia? To escape from the humiliation?'

'Nah. It wasn't until I got her younger sister stuck with a bun in the oven and their old man came after me with a World War Two .303 rifle.'

Detective Inspector Edwards faced the six uniformed officers in the squad room. The group consisted of a male sergeant, four male constables and one WPC. They all looked very unhappy.

'Let's go through it very slowly,' growled DI Edwards. 'Every one of you clearly remembers arresting Barry Simmons, right?'

They all nodded and muttered their assent. The sergeant said, 'There was no trouble. Simmons didn't put up any resistance and none of the Tug and Pullet regulars interfered. I thought it was pretty odd.'

'And you, Parker,' continued Edwards, 'clearly remember cuffing Simmons?'

'Yessir,' said Constable Parker.

'And then you took him out of the pub and put him in the van?'

'Yessir.'

'And there were four of you in the back of the van with him the entire drive to the station?'

'Yessir.'

'And you remember talking to him?'

'Yessir,' said Parker, 'he was taking it surprisingly well. Joking and all that.'

'He was telling jokes?' asked Edwards.

'Er, yessir . . .'

'About what?'

Parker exchanged a blank look with two of the other constables. 'Er, I can't remember exactly . . . but I don't think they were very good.'

'No wonder he was in such a bloody good mood,' snarled Edwards, 'because he wasn't even *in* the frigging van!'

They had no answer to that. Parker scratched his head. 'It certainly is a puzzle, sir.'

'Prat,' muttered Edwards. 'You were clearly all hypno-tised. And it must have happened at the Tug and Pullet. Do you remember anything odd happening?'

'You mean apart from Barry disappearing into thin air?' asked the WPC, innocently.

'I mean did you notice anything unusual happening in the pub?'

All but one of them murmured no. Edwards looked at the constable who'd said nothing. 'Yes, Harris? Did you notice something?'

'Well,' said the constable hesitantly, 'I'm not sure, but when I entered the Tug and Pullet I got the impression that the pub was the centre of a vortex of malevolent supernatural power and unspeakable evil.'

'Did you?' Edwards turned on the others. 'And what about you lot. Any whiff of malevolent supernatural power? A pong of unspeakable evil?'

'I thought it smelt a bit musty,' said the WPC, finally.

Edwards groaned. 'And you didn't spot the odd couple who were Simmons's accomplices on the raids?'

'No one in the pub fitted their descriptions,' said the sergeant.

'Right then,' said DI Edwards, firmly. 'You're going back to the Tug and Pullet and I'm coming with you. And if any bastard tries to hypnotise *me* I'll cut him off at the knees! Let's go!'

Travis looked at his watch. 'I suppose I'd better be getting home. Jack will want me to get back to work on that bloody screenplay.'

'You finding it hard yakka, mate?'

'Very hard yakka, whatever that means. I'm not cut out for that kind of writing. I'm a journalist. Or was,' he added bitterly.

'Might be able to help you out there, mate,' said Harry. 'I've been involved with quite a few screenplays in my time. A couple of them based on my own novels.'

'Really?' asked Travis, perking up. 'Did they make it onto the screen?'

'Sure. One of them even starred Elizabeth Hurley.'

'Gosh! That must have done the movie a power of good.'

'Nah. That was before she was *the* Elizabeth Hurley. She didn't go and get famous until about three weeks after the flaming film had disappeared from the West End.'

'Too bad.'

'Too right it was. Anyway, I'd be happy to give you a hand, mate.'

'Great,' said Travis. 'Maybe you could come round to my place tomorrow.'

'What's wrong with right now?'

'Well, to put it bluntly, we're both pretty pissed, Harry.'

'Perfect state to be in, when it comes to writing screenplays, sport,' said Harry, and fell off his bar stool.

*

Detective Inspector Edwards, followed by his six officers, stormed into the Tug and Pullet. He spotted Barry Simmons almost at once. Barry was standing at the bar large as life. His equally obnoxious brother Nigel was with him. Nearby the pair, DI Edwards thought he glimpsed a very tall man dressed in a black suit but when he looked again he couldn't see him.

As he ploughed through the throng towards the brothers he was astonished to see that they were counting a huge pile of money on the bar. Surely they couldn't be that bold . . . or that stupid. Then again, the extent of their stupidity was legendary in the area. He put a hand on each of their shoulders. 'Hello, lads! Having fun?'

They both turned and regarded him without concern. In fact they both grinned at him. 'Well, if it isn't DI Edwards himself,' said Barry. 'We're really honoured, aren't we Nigel?'

'Yeah, real chuffed,' said Nigel.

Edwards didn't like their attitude. It unsettled him. He pointed at the pile of money. 'This yours?'

'It is now,' said Barry.

'We won it on the lottery,' said Nigel and giggled.

'Truth is, we're minding it for a friend . . .'

'Whatever the story is, you're both nicked,' said Edwards. 'Sergeant, read them what laughingly passes for their rights.'

As the sergeant proceeded to do just that, Edwards produced his handcuffs and cuffed Barry Simmons to his wrist. 'I don't know what little trick you played last time, Barry, but you're dealing with me now.' Then to Constable Parker he ordered, 'You and Fenton collect all that money.'

While this was going on Edwards scanned the bar, looking for the two other men described by the bank robbery witnesses, but he couldn't see any likely candidates. Then he remembered the tall man he'd briefly glimpsed on the way in, but there was no sign of him now. Edwards wouldn't have minded betting that he was one of the men he wanted, but he could wait until later.

With Nigel Simmons cuffed to the sergeant and the money

99

collected from the bar, Edwards led the group through the pub towards the entrance. He half expected there to be trouble from the regulars but no one got in their way or said anything. On the contrary, there seemed to be a general air of amusement throughout the place. Even so, he was relieved once they were out on the street.

'You're wasting your time, Edwards,' Barry told him with a laugh. '*He* won't let you arrest us.'

'Who is this "he", Barry? Don't tell me you've found religion.'

'*He* is the Master. The new guvnor around here.'

'Oh yeah? What's his name?'

'Prince Valerie.'

That brought DI Edwards to an abrupt halt. He stared at Barry. 'You what? Prince *who*?'

'Prince Valerie. He and his sorcerer, Damion, are very powerful blokes.'

'I think I understand at last,' said Edwards bitterly. 'This is clearly National Talking Absolute Bollocks Day but no one told me about it . . .'

They all piled into the van and it began to move off. 'You want to tell me anything about your two mystery accomplices on those bank jobs, Barry?' Edwards asked Barry.

'I just did.'

'I don't follow,' said Edwards, puzzled.

'It was our new guvnor, the Prince. And Damion.'

'I'm sorry I asked,' sighed Edwards.

Edwards's superior, DCI Canterbury, was waiting in the docking bay when they got back to the station. As Edwards got out of the van with Barry, the DCI confronted him. 'Edwards, what is going on around here today? I'm getting reports that read like Enid Blyton on LSD! Stuff about people being turned into toads and small furry animals!'

'It's been an unusual kind of day, Tom,' said Edwards, having decided to go for the understating approach.

'And what's this I hear about you charging off mob-handed to pick up Barry Simmons?'

'Because he's in the frame for the bank jobs.'

'So where is he then?'

'Sorry?'

'Why have you come back empty-handed?'

Edwards was confused. 'But we didn't, Tom. We've got him right here. See. . . ?' He pointed at the grinning Barry Simmons and held up the cuffed wrists.

'Are you feeling all right, Edwards? All you're showing me is an empty pair of handcuffs,' said the DCI.

Edwards got a bad feeling in the pit of his stomach. 'You can't see him . . . or his brother, Nigel?' He pointed again at Barry and then at Nigel who was cuffed to the sergeant.

'All I can see is six uniformed idiots and a plain-clothed pillock,' fumed the DCI.

'Oh shit,' said DI Edwards.

'Told you so,' said Barry, and vanished. So did Nigel. The uniformed officers looked around in astonishment.

'It's bloody happened again!' gasped the sergeant.

Edwards groaned.

'Do you clowns want to tell me what you're playing at?' demanded the DCI.

'It's kind of hard to explain . . .' said Edwards.

With difficulty Travis managed to get the key in his front door and opened it. Unsteadily, he led Harry Adam Knight into the flat. 'Anybody home?' he called. 'Beatrice? Jack? Sharon?' There was no response but he could hear the TV playing in the living room. He went in. Beatrice was slumped on the divan watching TV. 'Hello, Beatrice, there's someone I want you to meet . . .'

'Shush,' she said without taking her eyes from the screen. 'I'm in the middle of *Brookside*.'

'Harry, meet Princess Beatrice,' said Travis. 'Our very own royal couch potato.'

101

'Pleased to meet you, your highnessness . . .' slurred Harry.

'Hello,' said Beatrice, still transfixed by the screen.

'She's a real little beauty,' Harry told Travis.

'Isn't she just?' he said, without enthusiasm. 'Beatrice, where's Sharon?'

'Still out.'

'Uh oh.' That didn't bode well for Stephen. 'And Jack?'

'Around somewhere. Probably hiding. Now shush . . .'

Ignoring her, Travis called out loudly, 'Jack, come here! It's okay! This guy's on our side!'

There was the sound of wings flapping and then Jack flew into the living room and landed on the back of the couch. He and Harry stared at each other. Harry said, 'Strewth, he's an ugly little bugger, isn't he?'

Jack said to Travis, 'Bloody hell, Travis, what did you do – stop off at the morgue on the way home for a takeaway?'

Travis sighed. 'The start of a beautiful friendship, I'm sure. Harry, meet Jack. Jack, meet Harry Adam Knight. He's going to help us.'

'I didn't know we needed a scarecrow,' said Jack.

'Hey, watch it, you little ratbag,' said Harry, 'or I'll flush you down the dunny.'

'Jack, Harry is a writer. He's going to help us with the screenplay . . .'

'Would you lot please shut-up,' complained Beatrice. 'I'm losing the thread of the plot.'

'Aren't we all?' muttered Travis.

Just then he heard the front door opening. It could only be Sharon because he'd given her his own spare key.

Sharon came into the living room. She looked dishevelled, as if she'd thrown her clothes on any old way, which she no doubt had. Sharon and dress sense would never be compatible. 'At last,' said Travis. 'And how did you leave Stephen? In a pile of neatly picked bones, I imagine.'

'He's perfectly fine,' she said, distractedly. She was sniffing the air. She came over to Travis and sniffed at him.

102

'Look, it's been a long day and I haven't had time for a shower yet,' he told her, annoyed.

She didn't answer but then went and sniffed at Beatrice.

'Hey,' said Beatrice and pushed her away.

'I thought so,' said Sharon, seriously.

'You thought what?' asked Travis worriedly. It was unlike Sharon to be serious about anything.

'I got a whiff of it earlier, when you came to Stephen's flat, but I thought I was imagining things. Now, I'm sure. You and Beatrice have been in his presence today.'

'*Whose* presence?' demanded Travis.

'Damion's,' said Sharon.

Chapter Thirteen

'Hypnosis?'

'It's the only possible explanation, Tom,' said Edwards.

They were sitting in the DCI's office conducting, or trying to, a post-mortem on the day's extraordinary events.

'You're saying there's someone in the Tug and Pullet who can hypnotise several people simultaneously?' asked DCI Canterbury incredulously.

'Yes, I am. And it's the same person who can convince a bank full of people that a teller has been turned into a small, furry animal.'

'A possum, wasn't it?'

'Whatever.'

'You're not suggesting that either Barry or Nigel Simmons are responsible? Those two morons haven't enough brain cells between the pair of them to make an amoeba.'

'No, they're just accomplices. The culprits are those two mystery men seen in the banks with Barry.'

'Any idea who they might be?'

Edwards shook his head. 'Barry came out with some crap about one being a Prince, though he had some kind of girl's name, and the other his sorcerer. Maybe they've been hypnotised as well.'

'That wouldn't be difficult. But I'm surprised that you were so easily manipulated, Ramsey. You don't remember anything at all?'

'No,' said Edwards. 'Nothing suspicious at all.'

'And no sign of these two strangers?'

'I thought I saw someone who fitted the description of the taller of the two when I first entered the Tug and Pullet but he . . . well, he just disappeared.'

'Hmmmm,' said the DCI, mulling it over.

'Tom, we need expert help. We need to call Scotland Yard and have them send us a police hypnotist right away.'

'I don't think there is such a thing.'

'Shit.'

'But I do know a police psychiatrist. He might be able to help. His name's Dr David Whiteman. He's based at West End Central. I'll give him a call . . .'

After a short conversation the DCI put down the phone. He looked perturbed.

'Wasn't he there?' asked Edwards.

'No. And he won't be there ever again by the sound of it.'

'What do you mean?' asked Edwards.

'Last night he piled up all his wife's clothing and possessions in the front garden of their home in Moor Park and set fire to them. Then he took off all his own clothes and danced naked round the bonfire while his wife had hysterics. When the Moor Park police arrested him he was gabbling on about demons, succubi and fairy princesses.'

DI Edwards stared at DCI Canterbury. Then, in shocked tones, Edwards said, 'Bloody hell! It's spreading!'

Travis sat up on the couch and moaned. He had the mother-in-law of all hangovers. Even his fingernails were throbbing. He staggered out to the kitchen, capable of movement only because the promise of a large glass of ice-cold orange juice spurred his limbs to a semblance of animation. He reached the refrigerator, opened the door and groped inside . . .

'If you're looking for juice you're out of luck.'

It was Jack. Travis hadn't noticed him sitting on top of the refrigerator. 'Don't tell me . . .' Travis groaned.

'Yeah, the girls drank it all. Tough luck. You look like something I once left on the cutting room floor.'

'Rats. I need Vitamin C. Desperately.' Travis poured himself a glass of water from the tap, drank it greedily and fell into a chair. 'Where are they?'

'Went out. Don't know where.'

'Great. They're probably knocking over another department store.' He put his head in his hands.

'Every little helps.'

'Don't even joke about it. And where's that writer I brought back last night?'

'In your study. He's either passed out or dead. Hard to tell which. Odds on it's the latter. Why'd you get involved with him?'

'It made sense at the time,' sighed Travis. 'He's had experience at writing screenplays but I don't know if he's any good.'

'I did a bit of checking up on his track record with Arnie,' said Jack. 'His credits include *Carnosaur*, *Bedlam* and *The Slime Beast*.'

'Sounds like the kind of movies *you used to* churn out. I would have thought you two were made for each other.'

'We just might be. He definitely has one thing in his favour – he's worked for Roger.'

Travis winced mentally at the cost of yet another transatlantic phonecall. 'Roger who?'

'Roger Corman, of course. The King of the Bs. The Master.'

'Oh, him again. I remember now. Your mentor.'

'And not just mine. He gave a lot of the big Hollywood names their start ... Coppola, Bogdanovich, Cameron, Hurd ...'

'Good for him,' said Travis quickly, wondering briefly if Douglas Hurd had got his start with Roger Corman, and why. 'So what did he and Harry do together?'

'*Carnosaur*. It was about genetically-engineered dinosaurs running amock ...'

'Oh, a rip-off of *Jurassic Park*?' asked Travis.

'Nah. Arnie filled me in on that. It seems that years ago your new buddy Harry wrote a novel with the same theme, called *Carnosaur*, natch. Roger bought it so he could make a legit competitor to *Jurassic Park*.'

'How did it do financially?'

'Arnie said Roger did really well with it. Made on a budget that wouldn't keep Spielberg in bagels for a week but Roger cleaned up in the video market.'

'So Harry must have made a fortune too . . .'

'He would have been paid okay but if he made a fortune then ol' Roger is losing his touch,' said Jack and cackled.

'Crikey, I feel rougher than an Abo's bark jockstrap . . .' Harry Adam Knight, the subject of the conversation, staggered into the kitchen. He looked like death cooled over. He sat down opposite to Travis and put his head on the table top.

'This reminds of a scene from a movie I made once – *The Corpse That Wouldn't Die*,' said Jack.

'I'm going to make some coffee,' said Travis, getting up. 'Want some, Harry?'

'Thanks, mate,' mumbled Harry from the table top, 'But I'd prefer a hair of the dingo that bit me. Hell, I'd prefer its whole bloody mangy coat.'

'That might be difficult,' Travis told him. 'I think we drank everything that was even vaguely alcoholic to the last drop last night. But I'll have a look . . .'

Travis returned to the kitchen with a Bells bottle in one hand and a thin wad of pages in the other. He held up the bottle. 'I can't understand this. There's almost half a bottle of whiskey left but I was sure we finished it.' He put the bottle and the pages down on the table. 'Tastes a bit funny though . . .'

Harry raised his head and stared at the bottle, then let his head slump back on the table top. 'Not surprised, mate,' he muttered. 'Got caught short during the early hours. Couldn't find me way to the dunny so I pissed in the bottle.'

Travis ran, gagging, to the sink.

Laughing, Jack said to Harry, 'Harry, I think I'm beginning to warm to you.'

'Oh, gwarrkkk!' said Travis from inside the sink.

Jack flew down onto the table and examined the batch of pages. 'Hey, you actually got some work done last night,' he said.

107

'Sure. I'm a pro, sport,' slurred Harry.

Jack started to skim-read the pages of the screenplay. 'This ain't bad either. But where did this sequence come from – the one where Travis seduces an entire team of nymph cheerleaders?'

'That's what Travis told me.'

'Hey Travis, I must have been asleep during that little episode,' Jack told Travis, who was now vigorously rinsing his mouth out.

'Artistic license,' spluttered Travis.

'More like a case of very sad wish-fulfillment,' said Jack as he continued to read through the pages. Finally he said to Harry, 'This stuff is okay. Consider yourself hired.'

'Whacko-the-diddle-oh,' said Harry from the table top. 'When do I get paid?'

'Well, we work on a deferred-payment basis here,' said Jack, lighting a Marlboro.

'Where have I heard that before?' groaned Harry. 'You bloody film producers must have the words ''deferred payment'' tatooed on your bums.'

Travis, his face ashen, returned to the table. 'I feel terrible,' he said.

'I'll second that,' said Jack, blowing smoke at him. 'You look so bad you're starting to make Harry here look half-alive.'

'And I'm worried too.'

'So what's new?'

'I'm worried about Beatrice and Sharon. Somewhere out there in London all by themselves.'

'Poor London,' said Jack and blew three linked smoke rings.

Detective Chief Inspector Tom Canterbury looked up from the report. 'A giraffe?'

'I'm afraid so,' confirmed DI Ramsey Edwards, reluctantly.

'But how did it fit in the bank?'

'With great difficulty, Tom.'

DCI Canterbury continued reading the report. 'Otherwise it's the same routine as before.'

'Yep. They got away with thirty thousand quid.'

'Ramsey, we're being made to look like complete berks. And by the likes of Barry and Nigel Simmons . . .' He shook his head.

'And their mysterious two accomplices. They're the brains behind all this – the ones we need to get our hands on.'

'We'd better do just that, and quickly. Area Command is going to start asking me awkward questions about this spate of bank robberies in our manor and I can't give them a report that includes stuff about bank tellers being turned into small furry animals . . .'

'And giraffes now, Tom . . .'

'And giraffes. I'd end up in the same padded cell as poor Doctor Whiteman.'

'Don't worry, Tom. Operation Nutcracker can't possibly fail.'

'You'd better be right.'

'I am, Tom. I've drafted in every available officer from the B Shift as well. Bugger the overtime bill. We're forming a watertight cordon round the whole Square. No one will get away when we launch Operation Nutcracker.'

'Then you'd better get cracking, Ramsey,' said DCI Canterbury, and smiled at his little joke.

Edwards didn't.

Beatrice and Sharon entered the Square and looked around. They were both in disguise. Beatrice was wearing a very short, black leather skirt, fishnet stockings, a low cut green blouse and was barely balancing on a pair of very high heels. Her hair was frizzed out, her mouth a gash of bright red lipstick and she was wearing sunglasses. Sharon was wearing a black jellaba and only her eyes were visible. Sharon lifted part of the veil, sniffed the air and said, 'He's in the pub. I can definitely smell him. And if Damion's in there, the Prince must be there as well.' She hastily lowered the veil.

'Are you sure Damion won't be able to smell you as well?' asked Beatrice worriedly.

'No. Not after I soaked this garment with Travis's aftershave. I bet I could get a whole lot closer and he still wouldn't know it was me.'

'But you're not, are you?'

'Er, no. Be silly to take an unnecessary risk.'

'So it's up to me,' said Beatrice, frowning at her. 'Alone.'

'Don't worry. You're soaked in Travis's aftershave as well. They won't be able to tell it's you. And we have to find out what they're planning . . .'

'I know, I know,' said Beatrice. She took a deep breath and then tottered off on her high heels towards the Tug and Pullet.

Chapter Fourteen

Damion was adding up figures on his recently acquired pocket calculator.

'How are we doing?' the Prince asked him idly as he surveyed the patrons of the Tug and Pullet. His loyal subjects. All thick as posts but then thickness went with the territory of being a royal subject.

'Not bad,' said Damion. 'Another ten thousand and we'll be able to afford that nice, converted split-level loft apartment we saw last night in Rutland Terrace.'

'Good. As grateful as I am to our new-found friends here, it will be good to be able to put some distance between us. They are rapidly becoming over-demanding, expecting me to solve all their problems.'

'Such as?'

'Well, for example, take Shirley over there . . .' The Prince pointed at a middle-aged blonde woman in a baggy cardigan who was seated at one of the tables deep in conversation with a younger woman. '. . . She's having an affair with Bernard who runs the local second-hand car dealership. She's worried that her husband, Alf, who has a vegetable stall in the market, will find out, completely unaware that Alf is having an affair with Mavis, Bernard's daughter who is already pregnant with Alf's child. Mavis, naturally, is terrified of the consequences when Shirley and her father find out the truth. She hasn't even told Alf so she's in a real state. I don't dare tell her, under the circumstances, that she's not Bernard's real daughter but in fact the illegitimate child of Bob, the road sweeper, who once had an affair with Sylvia, Bernard's wife, when she was a teenager. And there's Fred over there . . .' The Prince pointed again, this time at a chubby man of about thirty leaning at the bar. '. . . He's worried that his wife, Freda, will find out that he's squandered all their life savings on what was supposed to be a champion greyhound called Firefly, but he's now discovered that the dog only has three legs. Oh, and he's having an affair with Shirley too. On top of that he's picked up a dose of VD from someone – possibly Shirley – and he's pretty sure he's passed it on to Freda. He's not sure whether to tell Freda before he tells her about three-legged Firefly or after. Freda, of course, is having an affair too – with Shirley, who happens to be bisexual. Shirley, incidentally, is unaware that her son Mark has murdered his best friend, Grant, when he found out that Grant was having an affair with his mother. I tell you, Damion, these people and their damned problems are doing my head in.'

'You have my sympathies, sire, but there is a more pressing reason why we make ourselves scarce,' said Damion. 'After that visit from Beatrice and Travis yesterday we can't be too careful.'

The Prince shrugged. 'I think you too hastily jumped to conclusions. What do we possibly have to fear from those two?'

Damion was dubious. 'I don't know, sire. But I'd be happier if I knew more about this place.'

'No, on consideration I think it highly unlikely that he and Princess Beatrice have acquired dangerous new powers in this world. And you, Damion, have so regained your strength to the extent where you will be able to regain your power over Sharon.'

'Yes, sire,' said Damion, doubtfully.

The Prince gave a deep sign. 'Speaking of Beatrice reminds me how badly I could do with a woman right now.'

'You could have your pick of any around here, sire.'

The Prince's expression became pained. 'I don't want to sound a snob, Damion but . . . oh, what the hell, I *am* a snob and proud of it. I don't feel that any of the local women are in my league. Too common by half. Now Beatrice may have been a disloyal little bitch but she did have class, not to mention a right royal set of bazooms.'

'Pardon, sire?'

'Forgive me but this local vernacular is catching. I was referring to the Princess's breasts.'

'Oh, yes. I do recall they were rather impressive,' said Damion, adding hastily, 'not that I had the opportunity of a close inspection, sire.'

'It's all right, Damion. If I ever get my hands on her again I'll cut them off and turn them into money pouches . . .'

At this moment Beatrice tottered through the entrance of the Tug and Pullet and peered blindly around, her dark glasses reducing visibility of the pub's dark interior to near zero. She took them off and stared about.

'I still can't get over how she could have been so treacherous,' sighed the Prince. 'I was going to make her my bride and everything.'

'You're forgetting that "And everything" included eventually sacrificing her to the Lord of the Vampires,' pointed out Damion judiciously.

'Oh, *that*,' said the Prince, dismissively. 'Still no reason for her to stab me in the back and go off with that pillock.'

'Pillock?'

'Travis, Damion, Travis. About time you learnt some of the local lingo.'

'Yes, sire.'

By now Beatrice had spotted the diabolical duo, hastily put her glasses back on and began to make her way towards them. She reached the bar just in time to hear the Prince say, '. . . and after I've cut off Beatrice's breasts, I'm going to slowly gut her and then cook her intestines in a large iron pot while they're still attached to her and have them for lunch . . .'

'*Eeek!*' said Beatrice, involuntarily.

The Prince and Damion turned and looked at her. 'Did you say something, young lady?' asked the Prince.

Beatrice looked desperately around, then pointed to herself. 'Me?' she squeaked.

'Yes, you,' said Damion, staring hard at her. Then he started sniffing the air . . .

Beatrice shook her head. 'Nope. Not me.'

'I don't believe I've seen you around here before but you seem strangely familiar,' said the Prince. 'Are you a local?'

'A local? Me?' Beatrice gave a guffaw. 'Why, Lord love a duck sir, born and bred in Wilford Square all me life, duckie. Born within the sound of the Bow Bells, squire? . . . why, me dear old mum actually gave birth to me in the bell tower itself, it bein' rainin' cats and dogs at the time . . .'

Beatrice had taken the precaution of doing a little preparation before setting out on her mission of espionage.

'. . . me ol' man runs the eel and frog stand in the market. Er . . . any old iron . . . know what I mean?'

Unfortunately it actually *was* only a little preparation. The Prince and Damion stared at her in disbelief.

'Excuse me, your greatness, sir,' said Barry Simmons, tugging on the Prince's sleeve.

'What is it?' the Prince asked him irritably.

'The filth, your sireness, they have the place surrounded and they're closin' in . . .'

'Again?' sighed the Prince. 'Won't they ever learn?'

This one's a bigger operation, your wonderfulshipness. Lots of cops everywhere!'

'We can handle them,' said the Prince airily, 'can't we, Damion?'

'Sure,' said Damion, with a frown. 'How many is "lots"?' he asked Barry.

'At least fifty bodies,' said Barry, who was joined by his brother Nigel. Nigel was carrying a baseball bat, his small forehead puckered with concern.

'No problem,' said the Prince. 'Right, Damion?'

'Well . . .' said Damion.

But the Prince wasn't listening. He said to Barry, 'Do you know this peculiar young woman?'

Barry looked puzzled. 'Wot peculiar young woman?'

114

'This one right here,' said the Prince, turning. But she was no longer there.

With the distraction provided by Barry's arrival, Beatrice had seized the chance to duck out of sight and move hastily towards the front door. She had almost reached the entrance when the door burst inwards and policemen in riot gear began to pour into the Tug and Pullet. An officer with a loud hailer cried out, 'Everyone stay right where you are! You are all under arrest!'

Beatrice, trying to make herself small and insignificant, pushed into the wall of policemen. She thought she was going to make it until one of them grabbed her by the arm and growled, 'Where do you think you're going, darling?'

'St John's Wood,' she told him and kneed him in the groin.

'Right, you're nicked, bitch,' he moaned and flicked a handcuff over her right wrist.

Outside, Sharon was observing the proceedings with alarm. Not only was the Tug and Pullet surrounded by police but the entire Square had been cordoned off by back-up units. Like Beatrice, she tried to make herself inconspicuous but this was even more difficult to achieve when you were wearing a head-to-toe black jellaba. As she edged her way towards an exit road two officers barred her way with their shields.

'Well, well, what have we got here?' sneered one of them. 'Batwoman, is it?'

'Let me pass. I don't belong here.'

'You can say that again,' said the other officer. 'This is a dangerous patch for you to be in. The locals don't go much on Pakis. This is BNP territory.'

Sharon had no idea what they were talking about. 'Does that mean I can go?'

'Sorry, lady, but no. We have orders not to let anyone out of the Square. Now would you care to tell us what you're doing here?'

'Sightseeing. I'm a tourist,' said Sharon. 'From Tasmania,' she added as an afterthought.

'I don't care if you're Queen Lawrence of Arabia, sister,' said the first officer. 'You're not going anywhere.'

'Oh, I think you may be wrong there,' said Sharon, quickly pulled the jellaba up over her head and tossed it away. She wasn't wearing anything beneath it. The two officers stared at her in stunned silence. Then the second one said to her, 'Er, not that I'm complaining, Madam, but isn't doing this sort of thing against your religion?'

'Not *my* religion, it isn't,' said Sharon and stuck her tongue out at him.

The first officer picked up the jellaba and held it out to her, 'You'd better put this back on before we're obliged to arrest you for lewd behaviour or something.'

Sharon laughed and vanished.

The two officers looked at each other. 'Did you see what I just saw, Terry?' the first asked the second.

'Yeah . . . But then DI Edwards did warn us that we might see some weird stuff on this operation.'

'And he said we should try and ignore it.'

They were silent for a bit. 'Hard to ignore *that* though, eh?'

'I don't think I'll ever forget her,' said the second officer, Terry, wistfully.

Detective Inspector Edwards, in full riot-gear, had bellowed his warning over the loud-hailer for everyone to remain where they were in the Tug and Pullet, and for a few seconds it seemed as if he was going to be obeyed, but then everyone began running in all directions at once and suddenly the air seemed to be full of flying chairs and bar stools. 'Right, lads! Get them!' he cried as he warded off a missile with his shield. He spotted Barry and Nigel at the bar, as well as two strangers he'd briefly glimpsed before, and waded into the mêlée, using the loud-hailer as a baton. Whenever it made contact with someone's skull it made loud squawking sounds.

Then DI Edwards found himself facing Nigel Simmons. *At last*, he thought with satisfaction. 'Now, Nigel,' he warned. 'Be a smart lad and drop that bat.' At the same time he dropped the loud-hailer and drew his newly issued long baton. *This was going to be fun*, he told himself.

'Screw you, copper!' cried Nigel and swung the baseball bat at Edwards. Edwards parried the blow with his shield and prepared to strike back with his baton . . .

And abruptly found himself facing a giant aardvark. *Oh shit, here we go again*, were his last thoughts before the giant aardvark hit him on the head with the baseball bat.

Simultaneously, all his officers in the Tug and Pullet found themselves confronted with a mixture of bizarre creatures, some resembling real animals and others straight out of a perverse nightmare-land. Pandemonium reigned as confused and shocked officers tried to cope with the unnerving situation. One officer found himself struggling with a giant pink octopus, another faced his dead mother-in-law, a WPC exchanged blows with a giant Sooty the Bear, and the officer who was chased around the pub by Mrs Thatcher wielding a chainsaw would need counselling for years to come.

When the fighting broke out between the riot police and the Tug and Pullet regulars the Prince said irritably to Damion, 'Quickly, quickly! We're still visible to the idiots. . . !'

'Hold your horses . . . sire, there's a lot for me to deal with all at once . . .' He gestured with his hands and he and the Prince became invisible to the mortals in the room. Then, frowning with concentration, he prepared to unleash a mass spell. Finally, he gestured again . . .

The pub regulars saw nothing out of the ordinary aside from the fact that the police officers suddenly began acting very strangely, either dropping their batons and fleeing, or lashing out wildly at things that clearly weren't there. After a few moments of puzzled hesitation the regulars quickly began taking advantage of the situation, felling the confused officers with chairs and bottles.

'Good work,' said the Prince, sipping a glass of dry sherry as he observed the chaos. 'Better late than never . . . ooops, better take care of him, Damion.' The Prince indicated a

117

helmetless officer, blood running down his face, who was advancing towards them and blindly swinging his baton about in a dangerous fashion.

'Yes, sire,' said Damion and prepared to gesture . . . then he froze. 'It's Sharon!' he exclaimed. 'I can suddenly smell her! She's right outside in the Square!'

At that moment the officer's baton caught Damion on the side of the head and he dropped to the floor. Immediately all the police officers – those still standing – stopped moving and looked around, shaking their heads as if waking from a sleep.

'Oh shit,' muttered the Prince when he realized he was visible again. He started nudging the fallen Damion with the toe of his foot. 'Come on, Damion, up and at them, that's a good boy . . . Damion?'

A heavy, gloved hand fell on his upper arm. It was the officer who had felled Damion. His eyes were clear now and the Prince, with a sinking heart, recognised him.

'Right, matey, you're nicked!' bellowed DI Edwards.

Chapter Fifteen

Despite a splitting headache, DI Edwards was feeling pleased with himself. All in all it had been a good collar. Okay, so things had gone a bit wonky to begin with – he couldn't get that giant aardvark out of his mind – but in the end it had been a success. They'd got the Simmons brothers and their two mysterious accomplices, not to mention all the other villains who inhabited the Tug and Pullet. It had been touch and go for a few moments when he was arresting the taller of the two strangers. He had incredible strength and had actually snapped the chain on his handcuffs. Must have been high on drugs. It had taken six officers to subdue him, along with a few sharp taps with a baton to his head. Now he was in a restraining jacket after being pumped full of tranquillisers by a paramedic.

On the down side were the large number of casualties sustained by his officers. A lot had head injuries and a few were in a state of shock as a result of what they had experienced during the period when they'd all been . . . well, hypnotised or whatever. One of the worst cases was Officer John Parker. All he could say, over and over again was 'It was *her!* She was back and she had a chainsaw!' A broken man. Pity. He had been a good police officer.

A WPC approached him. 'Sir, the DCI has arrived . . .'

'Good,' he said and, taking care to avoid stepping on any broken glass, headed for the door. Outside, DCI Canterbury was just getting out of his car. 'Congratulations, Ramsey,' he told Edwards. 'I hear it all went to plan.'

'Thanks, Tom. There were a few hiccups but we came though in the end . . .' He stopped and frowned. He had just noticed the TV crews. They were filming a young woman who was handcuffed to one of the uniforms. What on earth was a prisoner doing giving press interviews? 'Excuse me, Tom, but I've got to sort something out . . .' He strode over to the group. 'What's going on here?' he demanded of the embarrassed-looking constable handcuffed to the girl.

'Sorry, sir,' said the constable. 'They all just gravitated to her. I told them they couldn't speak to her but they ignored me. And they won't let me past . . .'

'I'll see about that,' he said and turned to the TV crews. A woman interviewer was holding a microphone in front of the girl who was rabbiting on about something involving the royal family. He snatched the microphone out of the woman's hand. 'Alright, that's it! Show's over. You can't interview this prisoner!'

'Well, that's going to look good on the *One O'Clock News*. Nice one, Inspector,' the woman interviewer told him coldly.

'I don't care how it looks. Pack up your gear and shove off!'

Uncovered, the woman said, 'Would you like to tell the viewers the reason why this young lady has been arrested?'

'She's suspected of being involved in criminal activities,' he said, looking at the girl for the first time. He didn't recognise her which was odd because he thought he was familiar with everyone in the Square.

'Were you aware, Inspector' asked the interviewer, 'That she is a foreign national? And not only that, but a princess as well? You seem to have arrested a member of foreign royal family.'

Edwards gawped at her.

Travis was slumped in front of the TV set in the sitting room. His hangover hadn't abated and the aftertaste of the 'whiskey' lingered in the back of his mouth. He could hear Harry Adam Knight hard at work on the word processor in the study and Jack nattering away to someone on the phone in the kitchen, neither serving to improve his mood. And on top of everything, he had, half an hour ago, caught a commercial for

Prenderghast's new line of virtual reality helmets for children. The big launch was less than a week away and he didn't know what he could do to throw a spanner in the works. He had tried Prenderghast's office again and had got the same snooty secretary who repeated the story about Prenderghast being out of the country on business. He wondered if she knew who, or what, she was really working for. He was tempted to try and tell her the truth – Listen, Miss, do you realize your boss is one of the Dark Gods, and a major rat-fink to boot? – but decided against it.

He leaned back and closed his eyes. Too much to think about, too much to *worry* about. He wanted his old life back: his job, Heather . . .

The sound of a familiar voice tugged at his attention. And when he realized the familiar voice was coming from the TV his attention was fully engaged. He opened his eyes and sat up. 'Wha. . . ?' he said as he saw Beatrice on the screen. She was standing in front of a pub he recognised as the Tug and Pullet, dressed like a tart with very poor taste and appeared to be handcuffed to a policeman. There were a lot of other policemen in the background. 'Jack!' he yelled. 'Come here . . . quickly!'

'. . . And so,' Beatrice was saying into a microphone, 'I think it's a disgrace for your police to treat a visitor to your country in this fashion. And a *royal* visitor at that.'

Jack flapped into the room and landed on the back of the armchair. 'What's all the excitement? I was in the middle of an important call . . .'

'Shut up and look,' Travis told him, pointing at the TV screen.

'. . . and you are called Princess Beatrice?' asked the off-screen interviewer.

'That's right . . .'

'What did I tell you, buddy,' crowed Jack triumphantly. 'The camera loves her! She positively oozes on-screen charisma! Can I pick 'em or can I pick 'em?'

'Shush!' said Travis.

'. . . Yes, Samella. It's a very small country in, er, Europe.' Beatrice was telling the interviewer.

'Eastern Europe?'

'That's right,' said Beatrice and smiled a brilliant smile that lit up the screen. Travis could see what Jack was talking about. Her television presence was positively mesmerising. Who knows what effect she would have on a big screen.

The interviewer then asked her what she was doing in the Tug and Pullet and dressed like that. Beatrice gave her some waffle about travelling about incognito to soak up some of local colour. 'You see,' she said, 'I'm here in Britain to star in a movie. It's called *Damned and Fancy* . . .'

'Atta girl!' cried Jack, jumping up and down.

Travis continued watching with much less enthusiasm as Beatrice proceeded to tell the BBC and the public at large all about the film's writer and producer, one Travis Thomson.

'You're famous, dickwit!' chortled Jack.

'Yip, yip yahoo,' said Travis bleakly.

'Well, just don't sit there, go get her out.'

'Wouldn't it be simpler to just leave her in jail?' said Travis.

'You know you can't do that. And you've got to find Sharon too.'

'Yeah, yeah,' he sighed, and hauled himself out of the chair. What other option did he have, apart from changing his name and emigrating to Australia?

Detective Sergeant Dick Spencer met DI Edwards in the corridor. 'It's chaos outside, Guv,' he told Edwards. 'I've never seen a rat pack so big before. The media have gone berserk over this bloody woman. Even if we'd arrested Princess Di we wouldn't have kicked up such a fuss.'

'Tell me about it,' muttered Edwards. 'But we've got to hold her until we've checked out her story. No tourist in their right mind would go to Walford Square voluntarily. I'll question her later, after I talk to this Prince Val character. How is he?'

'Still pretty groggy but capable of being interrogated. He's in room three . . .'

'Right,' said Edwards, rubbing his hands together. 'Let's be having him then.'

Edwards sat down and stared across the table at the prisoner who was still wearing the heavy restraint jacket and was flanked by two burly uniforms. The prisoner glared at him even though his eyes were barely focused.

'I understand you haven't requested the presence of a solicitor,' said Edwards.

'Grrrrr,' said the prisoner.

'Good. As long as we understand each other. So let's proceed. For a start, what's your name?'

'Prince Valerie, ruler of the kingdom of Whiterose,' said the prisoner, his words slurred.

'Waitrose? Are you saying you own a chain of supermarkets?'

'I said *Whiterose*,' snarled the prisoner. 'It's a kingdom on the world of Samella.'

Samella? Wasn't that where the looney tunes woman had said she was from? So maybe she was mixed up in this after all . . . 'Do you know someone who calls herself Princess Beatrice?' Edwards asked him.

'Unfortunately. For a time we were to be married but then she turned against me.'

'Why?'

The prisoner shrugged, or tried to, within the restraint jacket. 'She discovered I was a vampire. I would have told her, of course, but I thought it best to wait until after we were married.'

'Yeah, wise move.'

The prisoner grunted.

Edwards leaned towards him. 'Look, can we cut the crap now? I don't know what your game is unless you're trying to make out that you're insane. If so, matey, it's not going to work with me. So stop all this vampire and prince and princess bullshit and tell me the truth.'

123

The prisoner's face reddened. He snarled. 'If your foul magic had not befuddled my senses I would break loose from these bonds and show you my true self. And then, as you begged for mercy in the face of my wrath, I would tear out your liver and consume it before your eyes.'

'If you fancy munching on *my* liver then you are bloody insane, matey,' said Edwards, laughing. 'Now come on, you prat, tell me the truth. The Simmons brothers have already confessed. They've fingered you and your little chum as the brains behind the bank jobs. Now I want to know who you are and where you've come from.'

'I've already told you that, dolt,' snarled the prisoner. 'But what of my sorcerer, Damion? Where is he? Why has he not come to my aid?'

'If you mean your little accomplice, he's in hospital, in a coma. Seems I rapped his noggin a little too hard. Sorry about that.'

'Never fear. Just another insult that you will pay dearly for, you peasant scum.'

'Yeah, yeah, yeah. Keep up this act as long as you want. I'm a patient man. And I know you and your chum are pros. You've even had your fingerprints removed. Now where were you operating before you moved into the Square?'

The prisoner didn't answer.

'Okay, here's what I know. For a start, you're not British. I can't place your accent but I would say you are from somewhere in eastern Europe. The same place as that weirdo woman, Beatrice, comes from.'

'After I eat your liver I'm going to parboil your scrotum.'

'Which means you're all in this together . . .' Edwards then had a flash of inspiration. 'Dick,' he said to DS Spencer. 'Go fetch the girl.'

'Sure, guv,' said Spencer and left. He returned shortly afterwards with the woman prisoner and a WPC. At the sight of the so-called Prince the woman paled. 'Valerie!' she gasped.

He smiled at her. 'Hello, Beatrice. How delightful to see

124

you again. Congratulations on your disguise. You had me fooled in the pub ... but only temporarily. I would have quickly realised who you were, and then ...'

She turned to Edwards. 'Are you mad? Don't you know who he is? Don't you realize how dangerous he is? You must lock him in your deepest, strongest dungeon and throw away the key!'

'I'm touched to see that your affection for me is as strong as ever, Beatrice my beloved,' the prisoner told her.

Edwards sighed. 'Look, I admit you've all got your act down to a T. I'll put you up for Equity membership myself. But it's a waste of time. I know who you two are.'

'You do?' she asked him.

'Yeah,' said Edwards and gave a triumphant grin. 'You're both part of the Russian Mafia!'

Travis saw, to his surprise, that a large crowd had gathered in front of the police station. Not just TV crews and photojournalists perched on step ladders, but ordinary members of the public, whatever they might be. All drawn to the place because of Beatrice's brief appearance on television. Extraordinary ...

As he got out of the cab he attracted a flurry of interest from the crowd, but when his face failed to register as belonging to anyone famous the interest quickly faded. As he prepared to push his way through the mass of people he felt someone grab his arm. He looked around. There was no one there.

'About time you showed up,' said Sharon, sounding irritated.

'Sharon? Is that you?'

'No, this is Audrey. Sharon couldn't make it so the Invisible Succubi Agency sent me as a replacement. Of course it's me, you twit!'

'Sharon, what happened? How come Beatrice got arrested? What were you two doing over here?'

'We were trying to find out what Prince Valerie and his

slimy toad Damion were up to but things went wrong. Beatrice got caught up in a police raid and got arrested.'

'So where are the Prince and Damion now?'

'The Prince is in this building. I saw Damion being taken away unconscious with a bad head wound. Hopefully it will prove fatal.'

'Prince Valerie is *here*?' asked Travis, alarmed. 'How have the police managed to keep him under restraint?'

'I don't know,' said Sharon.

'This is not good. The sooner we . . .' At this point he became aware that his conversation with the invisible Sharon was attracting unwanted attention from people around him. He quickly stuck a finger in his ear and started muttering into his lapel. Then he said loudly to those staring at him 'Radio mike . . . just talking to my boss . . .', but they still continued to stare at him as if he was crazy. Travis was getting used to being looked at in this way.

'Follow me,' Sharon told him.

'How?' he asked her, but the answer was plain when people in front of him were roughly shoved aside as the invisible Sharon ploughed into the crowd. Travis followed, muttering apologies as he went, hoping that some disgruntled individual, seeing only him to blame, would not take a swing at him. He reached the entrance to the police station which was barred by the solid presence of two male constables.

'Journalists are not permitted inside, sir,' one of them told Travis wearily, having probably said these same words over and over again. 'There'll be an official press conference later.'

'I'll take care of these two trolls,' whispered Sharon.

'No, wait,' he said hastily. 'Let me handle it!'

'Pardon, sir?' asked one of the PCs, frowning at him.

'I'm not a journalist,' said Travis quickly, reflecting, bitterly, that that was now probably the truth. 'I, er, represent one of your prisoners . . .'

'You're a solicitor?'

126

'Uh, no. I just represent her. I'm responsible for her. Beatrice. The, er, princess.'

They exchanged a glance. Obviously police-type information was being transferred in this exchange. Then the second one asked him, suspiciously, 'Are you *sure* you're not a journalist? You look like one. And you act like one.'

'I do?'

'Yeah. Shifty-like.'

'Yeah. Definitely shifty,' agreed the other one.

'Look, I'm Travis Thomson. *The* Travis Thomson. The one that Beatrice mentioned in her TV interview.'

'Anyone who saw that interview – any *journalist* – could say they're Travis Thomson, sir. Have you any identification?'

Travis got out his wallet. Unfortunately the first item to come into view was his National Union of Journalists membership card.

This provided one of the PCs with the opportunity to do his *Dixon of Dock Green* impression. 'Hello, hello, hello, what have we got here, sir?'

'All right, I was a journalist. Until recently. Now I'm a . . .' Travis lowered his voice, '. . . a film producer.'

'Oh yes?'

'Yes! And look . . .' he held out his NUJ card. 'See, it says Travis Thomson.' Then he got out his driver's license and displayed that too. 'Now can I see Beatrice?'

They exchanged another glance. Then one said, 'That's not for me to say, sir. But there's one person you'll definitely be seeing.'

'Who's that?'

'Detective Inspector Edwards. And he's really going to be happy to see *you*. Please come this way, sir.'

Chapter Sixteen

Travis sat in the interview room and nervously smoked a cigarette. 'The Prince is very close by,' said Sharon. 'I can smell him.'

'Why hasn't he used his powers to escape?'

'There's something wrong with him. He smells weak.'

'Good,' said Travis.

'I'm cold,' she complained.

'The heater isn't working,' said Travis. 'Probably on purpose.'

Sharon materialised. She was perched on the edge of the desk with her arms wrapped around herself.

'Is that wise?' Travis asked. 'What if someone should walk in and see you?'

'If I hear anyone coming, I'll disappear.' She reached over and plucked the cigarette from his fingers. She took a long draw on it and then said, 'You know how good my hearing is.'

At that moment the door opened and a young WPC started to enter the room. But when she saw Sharon she froze for a few seconds then hurriedly retreated, shutting the door.

'Your sense of hearing is positively supernatural,' said Travis.

'Poot,' said Sharon and vanished.

The door opened again. The WPC was back, this time accompanied by the duty sergeant who Travis had spoken with on the way in. The woman constable looked around the small room. 'She's gone!' she exclaimed.

'Something the matter?' Travis enquired innocently.

'This officer said she saw a woman in here with you,' said the sergeant. 'A *naked* woman.'

Travis raised his eyebrows. 'Oh really? In the habit of seeing things that aren't. . . ?' He stopped as he saw that the

WPC was staring wide-eyed at something above the table. He looked and saw it was his half-smoked cigarette floating in mid-air. He quickly snatched it from Sharon's invisible hand and put it in his mouth. The sergeant gave him a hard look.

'How'd you do that?' he demanded.

Travis shrugged. 'I'm an amateur conjurer.'

'Well, cut it out. There've been too many funny things happening around here recently.'

'Sarge, I don't feel well,' said the WPC who'd gone white. 'I'm *positive* I saw her.'

'Jenny, after some of the things I saw during the raid on the Tug and Pullet, a naked bird is a big improvement. Come on, what you need is a strong cup of coffee and an aspirin.' On the way out he pointed a warning finger at Travis. 'And no more funny business.'

'Yes, officer,' said Travis meekly.

When they'd gone Sharon reappeared. 'Why don't I shrink us both and then we can go and find Beatrice. I'll shrink her too and then we can sneak out of this place.'

'I don't fancy running around a police station a mere few inches tall. Police officers are notoriously clumsy when it comes to their feet. We'd end up looking like a pair of hamburgers. No, I'm going to have to try and persuade this Inspector Edwards character that Beatrice is innocent.'

'Someone else is coming,' said Sharon and vanished.

The door opened and a thick-set man in his mid-thirties strode in. He had a red face and thinning red hair. He also had a large sticking plaster on his forehead. Travis recognised him as the officer who had cut short Beatrice's television interview. He gave Travis a suspicious stare. 'You're Travis Thomson?' he asked brusquely.

'That's right,' said Travis, getting up. He held out his hand.

'Sit down. I'm Detective Inspector Edwards.' Ignoring Travis's extended hand he took the seat opposite. 'I'm going to record our conversation. Any objection?'

Travis sat down. 'I suppose not . . . but don't you have to charge me with something before you can do that?'

129

'Normally, yes,' said Edwards, switching on the tape recorder that sat on the side of the desk. 'And you have the right to refuse but I want to do this as a precaution.'

'Precaution?'

'I've just heard that a WPC saw something strange in here a short time ago, and then Sergeant Wells told me that you did some sort of trick with a cigarette. You told him you were an amateur magician, right?'

'Well, yes, but it's just a hobby . . .'

'Is hypnotism within your repertoire of trickery?'

Puzzled, Travis said it wasn't.

'Mr Thomson, we've been seeing and experiencing some pretty odd things around here recently. Hypnotism is the only possible explanation. I want the tape running just in case you try something. Then I'll have it on record. Okay?'

Travis nodded, thinking better of pointing out to the detective that if he was a hypnotist he could simply wipe the tape after hypnotising him.

'Right then, what's your connection with this Beatrice woman?'

'Um, well, I'm her host. I'm the reason she's in the country.'

'To make a film, right?'

'Yes.'

'So you're a film producer?'

'No . . . well, yes, I guess I am now.'

'What were you before you became a film producer?'

'I was a journalist. On *Watchdog* magazine.'

Edwards curled his lip. 'That leftie rag? Humph. So when did you become a film producer?'

'Pretty recently, actually.'

'How recently?'

'Very recently.'

'You just woke up one morning and said to yourself, hey, I'm tired of being a hack journo – I think I'll become a film producer.'

'Something like that, yes,' said Travis, though in different circumstances he would have complained about that 'hack journo' description.

'Interesting. Maybe tomorrow I'll wake up and say to myself, ''Gee, I'm tired of being a Detective Inspector in the CID, I think I'll become a master chef''.'

'It all sounds a bit unusual, I admit . . .'

'It sounds *very* unusual, matey.'

'I was talked into it by someone else. A veteran film producer. An American. His name's Jack DeSolva. He's made lots of movies.'

'For example?'

Travis tried to remember the titles of some of Jack's movies. He couldn't remember a single one. 'Uhhhhh,' was all he could say.

'He must be a pretty persuasive character,' said Edwards dryly.

'Oh, he is.'

Just then they both turned and stared at the door. That was because the door had just opened. Then it closed. But there had been no one there. No one visible, that is.

'Did you do that?' demanded Edwards, glaring at Travis.

'Me? No, of course not . . .' said Travis, though he could not help sounding guilty. And he wondered worriedly where Sharon was off to. 'How could I possibly open and shut that door from here?'

'That's what I'd like to know.'

'Maybe the station is haunted.'

'Yeah. And maybe someone is playing serious silly buggers. Let's get back to this Beatrice of yours. She says she's from some country called Samella. A country which doesn't seem to exist. Want to have a go at that one?'

'Sure,' said Travis, brightly.

'Go on. I'm all ears,' said Edwards and leaned back in his chair.

The invisible Sharon prowled through the station looking for Princess Beatrice, opening and shutting doors as she went.

She was amused by the reactions her investigations produced. Finally she located Beatrice, who was sitting looking morose in a small room. Sitting with her was the same young woman officer who had spotted Sharon before. Both she and Beatrice were holding cups of coffee.

Sharon walked over to the woman officer, who was staring worriedly at the door, and knocked her coffee cup out of her hand, with the result that her skirt became drenched. The young woman jumped up with a cry of distress, then said loudly, 'Oh shit!' and rushed out of the room.

Sharon materialised. Beatrice said, 'Oh, hello, Sharon. What are you doing here?'

'Trying to get you out,' said Sharon, sitting in the chair so recently vacated by the WPC. 'So is Travis. He's trying to convince some senior official that you're not part of whatever is going on.'

'Good for Travis. How's he doing so far?'

'Well, let's say that if you leave it to Travis you shouldn't accept any dinner invitations for the forseeable future.'

'Rats.'

'That's why I came to find you myself. Sooner or later Prince Valerie is going to regain his powers and we should be well away from here when that happens . . .'

'So, Samella is the old name for this little eastern European kingdom that got swallowed up by the Soviet Union?' said Edwards.

'Correct,' said Travis.

'And the bloke who calls himself Prince Valerie comes from the same place?'

'Correct again.'

'Presumably he was in the rackets back in Russia? Part of the mafia?'

'Oh, certainly,' agreed Travis, wondering what he was talking about.

'So what's the woman's connection with him? She working for him?'

132

'Beatrice? Definitely not. They were engaged to be married for a while but she broke it off when she found out he was a vampire.'

'He told me about that. So you think he's a vampire too?'

'No. But *he* thinks he's a vampire,' said Travis. 'Which is almost as bad as actually being one. He's very dangerous.'

'I'll keep that in mind. So what's he doing over here organising bank robberies?'

'I don't know anything about bank robberies but I would say his main reason for being in London is Beatrice. He's, er, rather upset about me taking her away.'

'Which brings us to an interesting point. How exactly did you bring Her Highness to Britain? Did you fly over to Russia and sweep her off her feet?'

'Not exactly . . .' said Travis.

'And how did you come to know about her?'

Travis thought for a while. Or tried to. He felt he was sinking in quicksand. It was now about up to his chin. 'I saw her in a movie. On Channel Four. A Samellian movie. Channel Four were running a season of Samellian films. They have a thriving film industry in Samella. I was immediately struck by her screen presence so I sent her an offer . . .'

'How?'

'By . . . fax,' said Travis lamely.

'By fax,' repeated Edwards. The words hung in the air like a fart, and just as embarrassing. Then the door opened again. This time it was opened by a visible person. A male police constable. He went over to Edwards and whispered something in his ear, then left.

Edwards stared at Travis with a strange expression on his face. Travis didn't like it. Finally Edwards said, 'Now that is intriguing. Very intriguing.'

'Oh yes?' said Travis, trying to sound unconcerned.

'I had that officer run a computer check on you to see if you had any ''previous'' and he turned up something interesting.'

'Oh yes?' he said again, all efforts at sounding unconcerned completely abandoned.

133

'A few days ago you were charged with assaulting a police officer during a fracas at the Soho Centre club.'

'Well, yes, but the charge was dropped.'

'True. On the recommendation of a Dr David Whiteman, a police psychiatrist.'

'Yes. Good old Dave.'

'You might be interested to know that "good old Dave" is being held under observation in a mental hospital.'

'Really,' said Travis, surprised. 'I thought Virginia Bottomley had closed all the mental hospitals down.'

'He's apparently still raving about fairy princesses and demons. And your name crops up a lot.'

Travis said nothing.

'Look, I want the full story,' Edwards told him firmly. 'And it had better not be anything like that load of bollocks you just gave me then.'

Travis sighed. 'Okay, I wasn't exactly telling you the complete truth . . .'

'You surprise me.'

'But one thing I told you was definitely true. Prince Valerie is very, very dangerous. And so is his companion, Damion.'

'Damion is in a coma at Bart's Hospital. And he's under police guard. As for this Valerie nutter, I admit he's unusually strong but we managed to subdue him after a bit of struggle.'

'You were lucky. You caught him off-guard. Look, he really is a vampire. And can turn himself into all sorts of nasty things. Big things with wings and very sharp teeth and claws . . .'

Edwards was regarding Travis with a look that came close to one of pity.

And then something came between them.

It appeared on the table. A small figure of a woman about four inches tall. Then it rapidly began to grow.

'Buggeration!' exclaimed Edwards.

The figure continued to grow. Travis recognised her as Beatrice. When she reached her full height she smiled down at him and said, 'Hello Travis. Thanks for trying to help me even if you were cocking it up.'

'I've been hypnotised!' cried Edwards, rising from his chair and backing away. 'I've been hypnotised *again!*'

Travis also rose from his chair and helped Beatrice down off the table. 'You haven't been hypnotised,' Travis told Edwards. 'This is real.'

'And so am I,' said Sharon as she popped nakedly into view. She walked over to the cowering Edwards, picked him up and plonked him back down in his chair. 'And Travis has been telling the truth about Prince Valerie and Damion. You don't know what you're dealing with. You should destroy them both!'

'None of this is happening,' said Edwards dazedly. 'It's all in my mind.'

'It's useless,' muttered Travis. 'Nothing is going to convince him of the truth . . .'

But at that moment came a tremendous crashing sound and the building shook. Then came the screaming . . .

'Valerie!' hissed Sharon.

Chapter Seventeen

The screaming continued and there were more loud crashes along with the sounds of pounding feet. Then the door of the interview room burst open and an officer in plain clothes thrust his head in. 'Ramsey! We have a . . .' He paused momentarily when he caught sight of Sharon, but whatever was going on out there obviously outweighed any questions he might have had about the presence of a naked woman in the interview room. '. . . a problem! That prisoner, the nutter . . . he's . . . you'd better come . . . we've already called for an Armed Response Unit. . . !' He disappeared. Edwards, wearing the expression of a man who had taken a wrong turning when going for a piss in a multiplex cinema and returned to find he was watching an entirely different movie with an unfathomable plot, got up and hurried out.

'We'd better get moving too,' said Sharon, pushing Travis towards the door.

'We can't just walk out of here,' he protested.

'Oh, I think we can,' she said, as she faded from view, 'I think they're going to be too busy with the Prince to worry about us . . .'

And she turned out to be right. No one paid them any attention as they walked through the station and into the reception area. Ouside it was different. The wall of media people was still there. As he, Beatrice and the invisible Sharon stepped outside they were met with a chorus of questions: 'What's going on in there?' 'What's all the commotion?' 'Who's screaming?' and so on.

Travis said something about there being a minor emergency with a prisoner but then the shout went up: 'It's *HER!* It's *HER!* It's the *PRINCESS!*' And then, as cameras whirred and clicked, came the cries of 'Over here, Beatrice!' 'Look this way, princess!' and 'Could you show us a bit more thigh, darlin'?'

Television interviewers and print journalists struggled to reach her. Travis was amazed at the amount of frenzied interest she had stirred up with her single TV appearance. Jack was right. On camera she was even more magical than in person.

A sweaty, beefy man with a swollen red nose elbowed his way to the front of the crowd. 'Princess, I'm from the *Sun*. I've been authorised to offer you fifty thousand pounds for your exclusive story . . .'

Travis said to Sharon, 'Testicles. Attack.'

The *Sun* man went down with a scream of agony as the invisible Sharon followed Travis's command.

Then he told Sharon to clear a passage for them through the crowd. It was like the scene in *The Ten Commandments* after Charlton Heston ordered the Red Sea to part, though albeit on a much smaller scale and without any visible matte lines.

As Travis and Beatrice followed in Sharon's wake, one man did get close enough to yell at Beatrice 'Princess, I'm an agent! Are you represented by anyone?!', but he was quickly swallowed up in the tangled mass of flying bodies.

Finally they got clear of the crowd and ran down the street, Travis frantically looking for a taxi. Miraculously, one appeared and stopped for them. They piled in. He knew Sharon was with them because she was sitting on his lap. 'Where to?' asked the driver.

Travis looked over his shoulder. The media mob were charging after them. 'Anywhere!' he cried to the driver. To his relief, the taxi pulled away and the feeding frenzy mob were quickly left far behind.

'Travis?' asked Beatrice.

'Yes?' he panted.

'What's an agent?'

After a pause, Travis said, 'Beatrice, there are some things in this world it would be best for you not to know about. Agents are one of them.'

*

Nurse Anne Petrie, nineteen years old and pertly pretty, strode briskly along the hospital corridor carrying a bedpan. Her pertly pretty face wore a frown because she knew she had drawn the short straw with this particular duty. None of the nursing staff liked dealing with the patient known only as 'Damion X'. There was something spooky about him. And the rumours going around that something very strange had shown up on his brain scan didn't help.

There was another reason she didn't like this duty. It was sitting outside 'Damion X's' room. It was Constable Chris Evans, who thought that God had done all the women of the world a really fabulous favour by presenting him into the world. As she approached the room, and PC Evans, she took a deep breath and prepared for the worst.

She wasn't disappointed. Hearing her coming, PC Evans looked up from his copy of the Sun and gave her a smug grin. 'You again, Anne? Can't keep away from me, eh?'

'Actually, we played spoof for this job and I lost,' she told him, which was true.

He laughed at the very absurdity of the idea as he rose to open the door for her. She wanted very much to bash him over the head with the bedpan but with the hospital's supply budget so severely slashed she couldn't afford to damage it. 'Thank you,' she said with gritted teeth as she entered the room. He made to follow her in but she pushed the bedpan against him. 'I don't need any help, thank you.'

'Hey, he's a dangerous criminal. You need me to protect you.'

She gestured towards the unconscious patient in the bed. 'I don't need protecting from someone in a coma.'

'He could be faking,' said Evans.

'Out,' she said, firmly. 'I can hear your Page Three bird calling you.'

Reluctantly, he closed the door, giving her another infuriatingly smug smile as he did so. *Stupid prat*, she said to herself as she went over to the bed. She put the bedpan down on the bedside table and looked at the monitor screen. All his vital signs were stable. She peeled back one of the patient's eyelids. He was still deeply unconscious. No change. Then she pulled the sheet down to the foot of the bed and checked to see whether the catheter was still in place. As before, she wondered how this strange-looking man had sustained such severe damage to his genitals. Then, expertly, she removed the used bedpan from beneath the patient . . .

. . . and screamed.

The bedpan and its contents fell to the floor. The door flew open and PC Evans rushed in, baton drawn. He looked around wildly. 'What happened? What did he do?' he cried, advancing towards the bed.

Nurse Petrie, shaking, could only point dumbly at the floor. Evans looked. He saw the bedpan on the floor, and sitting beside it, ears twitching, was a white rabbit.

'It's a rabbit,' he announced.

Nurse Petrie nodded fiercely, still unable to speak.

'Where did it come from?' he asked.

She shook her head fiercely.

He looked at her, puzzled by her extreme reaction to the rabbit's presence. 'What's the matter? You have a phobia about rabbits?'

She shook her head fiercely again, then pointed at the comatose patient and then at the bedpan.

He didn't understand. 'I don't understand.'

She managed to speak. 'The rabbit . . . it . . . was in the . . . the *bedpan!*'

He still didn't understand. 'You're saying you found the rabbit in the bedpan?'

'Yes, you silly berk!' she cried. 'And it was under the patient! I've seen a lot of strange things in bedpans since I've been a nurse, but never a white rabbit before!'

'Calm down,' he told her. 'It's perfectly plain what happened here . . .'

'Yeah,' she said, pointing at 'Damion X'. 'I have a patient who's shitting white rabbits. Happens all the time.'

'Nahhh, someone's just playing a practical joke on you. I know what you medical types are like.'

'We don't play games with patients, you moronic cop! And who's been in here since my last visit?'

'Uh, no one,' he admitted.

'Then explain *that!*' she demanded, pointing at the rabbit. The rabbit, who had pink eyes, stared back up at her and twitched its nose.

Just then the patient farted. Both Nurse Petrie and PC Evans turned and looked at the figure on the bed. Something white was wriggling between his legs. Then it took off into the air. It was a white dove.

They watched it fly around the room for a while and then Nurse Petrie said weakly, 'And you can explain that as well.'

Evans's police radio squawked into life. Evans answered the call. Nurse Petrie divided her attention between him, the white dove and the patient. She wondered nervously what would appear next from his nether regions . . .

Evans was talking into his radio: 'Yes . . . yes . . . *What?!* You're kidding! Oh, sorry, sir . . . yeah, yes . . . My God! . . . Then he did *what?!* Bloody hell! What, here? No, no sign yet, sir. Anything unusual here. . . ?' He paused and looked at the rabbit and the dove. 'Well, yes, I guess you could say that. What? Well, it's kind of hard to describe, sir . . . yes, I'll wait right here until backup arrives.' He signed off and looked worriedly at the patient.

'Is there a problem?' she asked him. 'I mean, apart from the one we have right here.'

'Yeah,' he said, distractedly. 'Back at the station. His mate escaped, and wrecked the place in the process . . . a lot of weird stuff went on, according to the sarge. But it's not just that . . .'

'Oh?' She just knew she wasn't going to like what he was going to tell her.

'The sarge said Prince Valerie knows where *he* is . . .' – he indicated the patient with his baton – '. . . and the odds are he's heading here.'

140

'Oh.'

Evans looked nervously out the window, which she thought was odd, then went to the door, opened it and looked up and down the corridor. 'Backup are on the way,' he told her. 'There's nothing to worry about.' But his tone of voice told her that there was plenty to worry about.

'How can one man simply break out of a police station?' she asked.

'A man?' he said and gave a funny laugh.

'What's *that* supposed to mean?'

'The sarge said that when he left the station he wasn't exactly looking human . . .'

'Oh, really! You're being silly . . .' She went and picked up the bedpan. Her intention was to open the window and use the bedpan to scare the annoying dove out of the room. But as she went to open the window the constable yelled, 'Don't touch the window!'

'Now what are you raving on about?' she asked, irritated and scared at the same time.

'The sarge said . . . said . . .'

Suddenly the patient groaned and sat up. 'Ow, my bloody head,' he groaned.

They both stared at him. He stared back at them. 'Who the hell are you two? And what is this place?'

'It's a hospital,' she told him. 'You're very sick.'

'You can say that again,' Damion said, touching his bandaged head. 'And I'm very pissed off.' He made to get out of the bed. Evans waved his baton at him. 'Don't move! You're under arrest! Stay right where you are!'

'Idiot,' said the patient and gestured with his right hand. Evan's baton promptly turned into a long French loaf. Evans stared at it stupidly. Nurse Petrie wished more than ever that she was a better spoof player, because then she wouldn't be where she presently was.

'Damion X' got out of the bed. 'Where are my clothes?' he demanded.

141

She pointed dumbly at the closet. Evans was still staring at the loaf of French bread he was holding.

The patient tore out all the various bits of tubing from his body, along with the sensors, strode over to the closet and began to dress.

'You can't leave,' said Evans in a weak voice. 'You're under arrest. You're not going anywhere . . .'

'And you're very unwell,' added Nurse Petrie.

Behind her the window shattered. She gave a brief scream as fragments of glass blew past her. Then she turned . . .

A large *something* that seemed to be made of smoke, but with gleaming red eyes, was pouring through the broken window. She screamed again. The *something* materialised into a tall man dressed in black. His eyes remained the same red colour. Nurse Petrie decided that screaming a third time would be a waste of time.

'Damion!' said the tall man. 'Are you all right?'

'No, sire. But I'm glad to see you again. Let's get out of here.'

'Presently, Damion, presently,' said the tall man, turning to look Nurse Petrie up and down. He licked his lips. 'But first, introduce me to this tasty little morsel.'

'I don't know who she is, sire. I've just woken up. I found her and this uniformed fool here in the room.'

The tall man began to move towards her, giving a teeth-revealing smile.

Evans, who had completely snapped, pointed his French loaf at the tall man and cried, 'Stop, or I'll shoot!'

Nurse Petrie's reaction was more effective. She slammed the bedpan hard into the tall man's face, having decided she no longer cared that much about the hospital supply budget at that precise moment. The tall man staggered back, his nose spurting blood. She then threw the bedpan at the surprised 'Damion X'. It bounced off his bandaged head with a satisfying *clang*. She raced to the door, flung it open and sprinted off down the corridor.

142

She got away.
Police Constable Evans was not so fortunate.

Chapter Eighteen

As the taxi pulled up outside Travis's block of flats he was relieved to see that there weren't any reporters gathered around the entrance. But he knew it would only be a matter of time before they tracked him down. There weren't that many Travis Thomsons in the London phone directories. And they were sure to have figured out that wherever Travis Thomson was they would find their flavour of the month, if not the year – Princess Beatrice.

'I'm hungry,' complained the said flavour of the month as they got out of the taxi.

'And I'm still very annoyed with you,' said Travis. 'Both of you. You must have been out of your minds to go to the Tug and Pullet.'

'It was Sharon's idea,' said Beatrice, petulantly.

'Hah! You agreed it was a good idea,' said the invisible Sharon, which made the cab driver give a start of surprise as Travis handed him the fare. Travis decided to distract him by giving him an unusually large tip. Give a London black cab driver a very large tip and he wouldn't notice a thousand ton asteroid hitting the Earth. 'Let's carry on this conversation inside,' Travis warned the pair of them.

But in the flat he was dismayed to see Stephen sitting waiting in the kitchen. There was no sign of Jack. Travis hoped he wasn't hiding in the fridge again. 'Hello, Stephen,' Travis said wearily. 'How did you get in?'

Stephen got up. 'Yet another warm greeting. An old Australian guy let me in. Very drunk he is. I came over when I saw you and Beatrice on the TV news. What's going on? And what's all this crap about you being a film producer?'

'It's true,' sighed Travis. 'Sort of.' He put down the plastic bag he was carrying on the table. There was a clink of bottles.

He'd made the wise precaution of stopping at an off-licence on the way home.

Then, as Beatrice entered the kitchen, a strange change came over Stephen. He blushed and said awkwardly. 'Er, hi, Beatrice. I mean, princess . . .'

'Hello, Stephen,' she said disinterestedly, and sat down. 'I'm thirsty. And I'm still hungry.'

Travis noticed how Stephen was regarding her with a kind of awed expression. He hadn't looked at her in that way when he'd met her before even though he had been clearly taken by her beauty. Travis guessed that the spell she cast through the TV screen had claimed another convert.

Then Stephen looked around and said, as an afterthought, 'Where's Sharon?'

'Oh, she's around somewhere,' said Travis. He poured Beatrice a glass of mineral water and two large scotch and sodas for himself and Stephen. 'As for food we'll order a takeaway later,' he told her. Just then Sharon emerged into the kitchen from the bedroom wearing a dressing gown. She yawned theatrically. 'Hello, Stephen.'

He started at her. 'Where did you come from?'

'The bedroom,' she said, giving him a peck on the cheek. 'I was having a nap.'

'But the flat was empty when I got here apart from that Aussie guy,' protested Stephen.

'If only . . .' muttered Travis.

Sharon shrugged. 'I was under the duvet. You must have missed me.'

He shook his head. 'Impossible.'

The phone rang. Travis picked it up with misgivings. It was the mysterious Arnie for Jack. 'Sorry, he's not here at the moment,' Travis told Arnie.

There was a flapping of wings. Jack flew into the kitchen and angrily grabbed the phone from Travis. 'Give it here, dickwit! It's important.'

Stephen's glass slipped from his fingers and shattered on the floor.

Travis said, 'I'd better get you another one, pronto. You're going to need it.'

Then, Harry Adam Knight shambled into the kitchen, sniffing the air. 'Is that booze I can smell? You beauty, bottler! *Whacko-the-diddle-oh!*'

Elsewhere in London, another person was nursing a large, much-needed scotch. It was Detective Inspector Edwards. He was sitting in DCI Canterbury's office. The DCI was also nursing a large scotch. Both men were looking extremely despondent.

'Tell me again it didn't happen, Ramsey,' pleaded the DCI. 'Any of it.'

'None of it happened, Tom,' said Edwards. He had a brochure from the local council's Adult Education Department open on his lap. He had pencilled a ring around the Night Cookery Classes heading.

'But it did, didn't it?' sighed DCI Canterbury. 'So what am I going to tell Area? They're on my back for a full report.'

It was true, he'd always been a dab hand in the kitchen, thought Edwards, *whenever his wife actually let him into the kitchen, that is . . . Maybe, after he'd taken the course he could open a small restaurant . . .* 'Hypnosis,' he said, automatically.

'Don't give me any more of that hypnosis bullshit, Ramsey,' snapped DCI Canterbury. 'Hypnosis doesn't explain that bloody great hole in the skylight on the roof. Nor does it explain what you and several other officers witnessed this afternoon! Nor does it explain that this station was half-wrecked and five officers put into hospital!'

'Six, if you include PC Evans,' said Edwards.

'Oh yes,' said Canterbury, his face sombre. 'How is the poor lad?'

'Last I heard they were still operating.'

'Tsk, tsk. Terrible. How anyone could possibly do that with a French loaf is beyond me.'

'Yeah, but it could have been worse. It could have been his truncheon.'

After a few moments' silence, DCI Canterbury said, 'So what are we going to do?'

'Lie, Tom. Lie for all we're worth. It's our only way out.'

'But so many officers saw what happened, Ramsey . . .'

'And you think any of them will make an official report to that effect? It would be a one-way express ticket out of the force.'

'Don't I know it,' sighed Canterbury.

'And no one will tell the truth to the media either,' said Edwards. 'You can bet on it.'

'Ah, yes, the media. As irksome as it is to admit it, we have reason to be grateful to that "princess" person. She completely diverted the rat pack.'

'Yeah, I guess she did,' admitted Edwards grudgingly. 'But I don't like the way she and that Travis Thomson character just walked out of here.'

'Everyone was rather occupied with more pressing matters at the time,' Canterbury pointed out dryly.

'Well, she should be pretty easy to track down. We find Thomson and we'll find her.'

'Yes, Ramsey, but the point is – do we *want* to have anything more to do with her.'

'Leave well enough alone, you mean?' asked Edwards. 'Not very professional, Tom.'

'Do you want a repeat of what happened here today?'

Edwards thought about it. 'No,' he said and glanced at the Council brochure again. Maybe he could open a little trattoria when he'd finished the course. He'd always liked Italian food.

'You know, Ramsey,' said the DCI wistfully, 'I only joined the force because it was a family tradition. Originally I'd wanted to be a tree surgeon.'

'Really?' said Edwards.

'I've been thinking . . . it's not too late. If I took early retirement and went on a retraining scheme . . . But I suppose you think I'm being silly?'

'Not at all,' said Edwards, sincerely.

Stephen couldn't take his eyes off Jack, who was still on the phone. He was regarding him with horrified fascination. 'You're telling me he's an actual *demon?*'

'Well, he is now,' said Travis. 'Originally he was a film producer. I guess there's a difference.'

Stephen took another drink. 'I'm finding all this hard to take in.'

'I don't blame you,' said Travis. 'But there's a lot more. Sharon, for example.'

'Sharon?' said Stephen, looking at her.

'She's a demon too. A succubus to be exact.'

Sharon, holding a cup of coffee, gave Stephen a mock innocent smile.

'I don't believe it,' said Stephen.

'Show him one your party tricks, Sharon,' Travis told her.

'Sure.' She put her cup down, stood up and took off her dressing gown. A brief glimpse of glorious nakedness ... then she vanished.

The glass again fell from Stephen's hand. As it shattered Travis reflected that at this rate he was going to run out of crockery. Sharon reappeared, put the gown back on and sat down.

'She can also eat men's souls,' Travis told the stricken-looking Stephen as he fetched him a fresh glass and poured him another large drink. 'During love-making.'

'But ... but ...' he stammered. 'She and I ... we ... we ...'

'I know,' said Travis. 'I did try to warn you.'

'Don't worry,' Sharon told Stephen. 'I only had the smallest of nibbles.'

Stephen didn't look reassured. 'But where did they *come* from?' he demanded.

'A world called Samella. Beatrice as well. And Jack. Though Jack actually comes from California.'

'Beatrice is a demon as well?' cried Stephen.

'I am not!' she protested. 'I'm a princess!'

Just as Jack finally put the phone down it rang again. Jack snatched it up. Then said, annoyed, to Beatrice, 'It's for you.'

Travis watched mystified as Beatrice got up and went to the phone. Who could possibly be calling her?

'Oh, hello Philip,' said Beatrice into the phone. '. . . Yes . . . yes . . . oh, I'm sure you're right. Yes, I'll tell him. Thanks. Bye.' She hung up and returned to the table. 'That was Philip,' she told Travis.

'And who is Philip?' he asked.

'Philip Billson. He's my agent. He wants to have a meeting with you. Tomorrow. At his office. It's in Bond Street. I'll give you the address.'

'Your *agent?*' said Travis. 'You don't have an agent.'

'Yes I do. I just told you I did. His name is Philip Billson.'

'How could you possibly have an agent?' asked Travis.

'That man who approached me in the crowd outside the police station. He managed to slip his card into my jacket pocket. I found it and called him on your mobile while you were in that shop buying all those bottles of drink. He told you were exploiting me and that he could help me make a fortune.'

'I'm exploiting *you?*' asked Travis, blankly.

'That's what he said. Anyway, he's my agent now and he wants to talk to you tomorrow to discuss terms.'

'Terms?' said Travis.

'As much as I hate to admit it,' said Jack, 'You've got to admire the guy. He's right. She's an amazing commercial media commodity with a potentially huge earning power. And he's got in first. My hat's off to him.'

'Shut up, Jack. Beatrice. I'm not exploiting you. You don't need an agent.'

'He said you'd say that,' said Beatrice, smugly.

'Beatrice, he's an *agent!*' cried Travis in exasperation. 'He would say that!'

'And he said you'd say that too,' she told him.

Travis gave up and had another drink of scotch. He thought about taking up alcoholism professionally.

'I had an agent once,' slurred Harry Adam Knight, who had obviously taken the same decision ages ago and stuck to it ever since. 'I think,' he added.

'Some of my best friends back home are agents,' said Jack, defensively.

'I'm sure they are,' muttered Travis.

Stephen was still staring aghast at Sharon. 'You eat souls . . . during love-making?' he said in a weak voice.

'I told you,' she said. 'I've only had a nibble at yours.'

'She's also a pretty good cook,' Travis told him. 'You could do worse.'

Chapter Nineteen

Travis sat in his study watching Harry Adam Knight work at the keyboard of his computer. He had noted that Harry's hands weren't shaking so badly this morning despite the fact that he had consumed the usual copious amount of scotch the night before.

It had been a hectic two weeks since the incident at the police station. Much had happened. Princess Beatrice had become a media superstar, with the result that there was a permanent gaggle of press and TV people camped outside his block of flats. Beatrice had become so famous that there were rumours that Princess Diana was planning to sue for loss of attention. Thanks to Beatrice all the money for the film had been raised remarkably quickly, though also thanks to Beatrice, or rather her agent, the budget had doubled to pay for her required fee.

Having been accused of exploiting Beatrice by her bloody agent Travis had decided to do just that by having her make a statement, during one of her many TV appearance, to the effect of warning the public not to buy Prenderghast's virtual reality helmets for their children. The effect of her warning had been dramatic – the sales campaign had been stopped in its tracks overnight and the device had been withdrawn from the shops before its official launch. There had been some bleating from a spokesman for Prenderghast's company and vague threats of legal action but so far nothing had materialised. Travis knew that wherever he was, Prenderghast was far from happy with him and there would be consequences to face, but for the time being Travis didn't give a shit.

One unusual development had nothing to do with Beatrice, instead it was Sharon's fault – Stephen was in the process of converting to Roman Catholicism with the long-term aim of becoming a priest.

Sharon, meanwhile, at Travis's instigation, was having torrid affairs with several *Sun* journalists. He had lifted the no-soul-eating rule but she had so far reported slim pickings in that area.

Other amusing fallout from Beatrice's mega-fame: Travis's ex-editor, Martin Shulman, had rung him up after Beatrice's warning broadcast about Prenderghast's VR helmets and offered him his old job back; and Heather, his ex-girlfriend, had rung him and suggested they have lunch together today. Travis had turned down both offers, though he had been sorely tempted by the latter one. Maybe some other time, in the future . . .

'We're in the last furlong, sport,' announced Harry Adam Knight. 'Ten more pages and the final draft will be finished . . .' He leaned back and stretched, then took a sip from the glass of chilled vodka and orange juice – which he referred to as his morning 'health drink' – which sat by his elbow.

'Good,' said Travis. 'Jack will stop giving us grief. I didn't think he could become more annoying than he used to be but power has gone to his head. Little creep.'

'Ah, don't be too hard on Jack,' said Harry. 'For a demon he's okay. I've worked for worse.'

'That's hard to believe,' said Travis.

'Nah, back in Oz I worked for a bastard of a film producer who locked me in my hotel room until I finished his bloody screenplay. The nong had the nerve to have the mini-bar removed and banned me from using room service. I almost died.'

'Sounds awful,' said Travis. 'Tell me, Harry, don't you ever feel homesick for Australia?'

'Nah, sport. Had me fill of the place when I lived there. Compared to this place there's too many things out there determined to do you in or cause you maximum aggravation. Things like snakes, spiders, flies, mozzies, sharks and Aussie women. And if you go for a brief walk in the sunshine you came back covered in malignant carcinomas. Give me old Blighty any day. I've been here over twenty years and never seen the sun once.'

'Really?' said Travis, though he wasn't too surprised by this item of information.

'I'll tell you for nothing, sport, I was lucky to get out of Oz alive. Call me a paranoid old galah, but I'm sure that country had it in for me. I had more than a few narrow escapes when I was sure it was going to be stiff bikkie time for old Harry.'

'Such as when?'

'Well, there was the time I was working as a pilot for the Royal Flying Dental Service. The dentist I was chauffeuring around was a sheila called Doctor Raylene DiMaggio. Bonzer-looking little hornbag she was, but though I tried my hardest to get into her panty zone I had as much luck as a koala bear in a bush fire. Anyway, one day, when I was flying her out on an emergency call – some poor bastard in a mining camp had had his teeth knocked out during a political debate in the camp bar – we had a bit of engine trouble. It stopped working. Truth is, I had a pretty bad hangover that day and had forgotten to fill the tank, but bugger me if I was going to tell Doctor Raylene that. So we went down . . .'

'You crashed?' asked Travis.

'Well, sport, I'd prefer to describe it as a controlled emergency landing. However the plane was a total write-off. We were both okay, though, apart from severe bruising and a bit of concussion. The radio was history so we couldn't call for help but the doc wasn't too worried – she said if we waited by the plane the search party would soon find us. I didn't have the heart to tell the poor sheila that apart from forgetting to fill the tank I'd also forgotten to file my flight plan before leaving the base, so no one back there would have had a clue as to which way we went.

'We'd come down in the Manguiup Desert, one of the most hottest and arid places in Oz, but if the days were hot the nights were colder than a tax inspector's heart. So that night

153

as we lay shivering next to the wreckage I suggested that a bit of close body contact might not go amiss, survival-wise. She agreed, kind of reluctantly, and naturally when I tried again to make a foray into her panty territory she told me what I should have suspected – she took her vacations on the island of Lesbos, if you get my meaning. Yeah, just my luck to be alone in the middle of nowhere with a gorgeous sheila who shared my own interest in gorgeous sheilas!'

'Tough luck,' sympathised Travis.

'I tell you mate, I felt as low as a pair of snake's testicles. So considering the situation I said I was going to find help. She said it was suicidal but I knew that unless I did neither of us stood a chance of attending another barbie. So I took off with half the water while she stayed with the plane. Then the sun came up and pretty soon I was as tuckered out as a pom garbage collector.

'The water soon went and my prospects of getting through alive were as grim as a toilet on a pommy cross-channel ferry. My brains started to fry and I could feel life ebbing away. I collapsed onto the sand and that's when I had one of those "near-death" experiences that I'd read about in the Australian Reader's Digest magazine. You know what I mean, when you see a white glowing tunnel leading to Surfer's Paradise or some other holy environment. I could hear voices from other members of the Knight family tribe who had already fallen off the twig calling me to enter the tunnel and join them. That really scared the shit out of me because all my dead relatives had been boring ratbags and I didn't fancy spending five minutes with them, let alone eternity . . .

'Then I heard a voice I didn't recognise. I opened my eyes and saw that standing over me was a two-headed Abo. "Bloody hell!" I cried. Obviously the fallout from all those pom atom tests in the desert back in the fifties had been more serious than I realized. Either that or my frazzled brain cells had gone walkabout . . .

'But it turned out that the two-headed Abo was an extra from a film being made in the area. It was an Australian-

American-Taiwanese co-production called *Crazy Kelly vs the Time Guardians*, and was, from what I later saw, a pile of sci-fi bulldust about Ned Kelly – an Oz national hero – who gets sucked into the future, thanks to his steel helmet, and has to do battle with a bunch of alien wankers dressed in costumes that must have been run up by some Paddington – the New South Wales version – poofter with his lights out.

'Not that I could really complain. The film company had just lost their Best Boy – he'd been run over by a camel the week before – so they hired me as a replacement ... And when the producer found out I was a dab hand with the old quill and parchment I ended up doing rewrites on the dialogue, which ended up being my introduction into the script-writing game. My career with the Royal Flying Dental Service was certainly down the dunny pan so it all turned out for the best in the long run ...

'But what happened to the woman dentist?' asked Travis.

'Oh, she was okay. By the time I'd put a call through to the base she'd already been found by a party of Japanese surveyors planning out a golf course. Do you know, it's estimated that by the year 2010, eighty six percent of the land area of Oz will be covered by Jap golf courses?'

'No, I didn't,' Travis told him.

Jack flew into the study. 'Hey, you guys! She's on again! Come watch!'

Dutifully, Travis and Harry followed Jack back into the living room. On the TV they saw Beatrice, looking as magically radiant as ever. She was a guest again on the *Nick and Judy Show*, or was it the *Anne and Richard Show*? Travis could never tell the difference. To him it was all the same thing – synchronised simpering.

Beatrice was in the process of describing her childhood in the poor Eastern European country of Samella, how she spent her childhood on a collective potato farm, how she was discovered as teenager by the great Samellan film director Ruger Kormannis, and, after appearing in a number of his films, became Samella's best-loved film star. Travis had heard this routine before, though the details varied each time, and was still surprised that people swallowed any of it. A couple of journalists had dared to point out that they could find no other reference to Ruger Kormannis and his films, nor even any reference to the country of Samella itself, but no one paid them any attention, such was the extent of Beatrice's magical influence via the TV cameras.

Judy, or was it Anne?, asked her how her first English-language movie, *Damned and Fancy*, was coming along. Beatrice told her that they hoped to start shooting at the end of March even though they hadn't completed the casting yet. But she had heard that Tom Cruise was close to signing up as the leading man . . .

'Tom Cruise is going to play *me?!*' exclaimed Travis.

'It's on the cards but unlikely,' said Jack, eyes fixed eagerly on the TV screen. 'Makes good copy though. Atta girl! We're really going to clean up with this movie!'

Someone is, thought Travis, a trifle bitterly, *but it probably won't be me*. He wondered if he should get an agent as well.

'She's providing us with thousands of dollars of free publicity!' cried Jack excitedly.

'True,' said Travis. 'But the more publicity we get the more exposed I feel.'

'Hey, the police have left you alone, haven't they?'

'Yes, but it's not just them I'm worried about. I'm thinking about Prince Valerie and Damion.'

'Relax,' Jack told him. 'They probably don't even own a TV set.'

But at that precise moment Prince Valerie and Damion were indeed watching Princess Beatrice on the same TV programme. They were in the vast sitting room of their docklands penthouse. They'd given up trying to raise money by continuing the risky business of robbing banks; instead they'd come up with the safer strategy of picking a suitable property and then, by using Damion's powers of suggestion, had simply persuaded the present owners to sign the flat and all its contents over to them. The ex-owners had then developed an overwhelming urge to move to Guatemala.

Prince Valerie hissed at Beatrice's image on the screen. 'Let the little bitch have her moment of glory in this world,' he snarled. 'As soon as you've fully recovered,' he told Damion, 'and regained all your power we will strike. We will smite her such a smite that she will know the meaning of real pain and terror. And we will similarly smite her friends too.'

'And we'll especially smite Sharon,' said Damion, and gave an evil chuckle. 'Heh, heh, heh, heh, heh, heh, heh . . .'

Prince Valerie gave an even more evil chuckle, 'Heh, heh, heh, heh, heh, heh, heh, heh, heh, heh, heh, heh, heh, heh, heh . . .'

Travis was sitting in the kitchen having lunch when the phone starting ringing. He ignored it, presuming it would be for Jack. He was surprised when Jack flew in and told him the call was for him.

'A phone call for me! In my own flat! What a novelty!' he said as he picked up the telephone. 'Hello?'

'Mr Travis Thomson?' asked a woman's voice that he vaguely recognised.

'Speaking,' he told her.

'This is Mr Prenderghast's secretary . . .' she told him.

'Oh, hello . . .' he said. *Uh oh*, he thought.

'Mr Prenderghast is now back in the country,' she said.

'He is?' *Was it time for panic stations?*

'He is. And he wants to see you. Today.'

Yes, it was definitely time for panic stations.

Chapter Twenty

'I'm doomed,' said Travis, not for the first time.

'It's your fault,' said Jack. 'I warned you not to fool around with Prenderghast's VR helmet campaign.'

'I couldn't sit back and let him get away with it! He was going to suck the life force out of this country's children!'

'Who'd have noticed?' asked Jack.

'I had to do what I did,' said Travis, taking a large swallow of scotch and soda.

'Well, hooray for you, Hopalong Cassidy. And now you're in deep shit as a result.'

Travis paced up and down the kitchen. 'There's no way out. If I don't go to his office he'll come *here*.'

'Yeah. You can't hide from Prenderghast. I know that for a fact.'

'Good grief . . . when I simply threatened him he sent me to Samella. Now that I've buggered up his entire operation what do you think he has planned for me?'

'You don't want to hear my opinion on that one, believe me,' said Jack.

Travis glanced at his watch. 'Oh God, I'd better get moving. His secretary said I had to be there by three.'

'Good luck. And could you do me a favour when you see Prenderghast?' said Jack.

'What's that?'

'Don't mention my name.'

Travis grunted. 'So much for solidarity.' He went to the bedroom to get his coat. As he was about to shut the wardrobe door he noticed the .45 automatic that was sitting on the shelf wrapped in a towel. He'd forgotten all about it. He picked it up and gingerly unwrapped it. It looked big and sinister. Just like Prenderghast.

He took it out into the kitchen and showed it to Jack. 'I'm going to take this with me,' he said.

'Oh, that's just brilliant, dickwit,' groaned Jack. 'What good would that do against Prenderghast? Besides, it's *his* gun. He magicked it up. You even point it at him much less try and fire it and it's liable to blow up in your face.'

'Perhaps,' admitted Travis. 'But I still feel better having it with me. And you never know, maybe I can use his own magic against him.'

'In your day dreams.'

'Maybe . . .' sighed Travis as he tucked the weapon into his waistband under the coat. 'But it's better than nothing.' He took a deep breath. 'Well, here I go. Wish me luck.'

'Good luck, Travis,' said Jack. 'You poor, doomed, completely fucked-up loser.'

'Thanks, Jack. I appreciate that.'

On arriving in the Docklands area, Travis promptly got lost in its confusing maze of roads. He noticed he kept passing the same buildings and realized he was driving round in circles. He remembered now that he had had trouble finding Prenderghast's headquarters on his fateful previous visit – a mere few weeks ago in this world but many months ago as far as Travis was concerned. He found a parking space, pulled up and got out his map. His old self had put a cross on it to mark the building's location. Fine. Now where was he now in relation to it? He looked around for a street sign and, miraculously, found one. He was, he saw, in Byng Street. And then, looking again at the map, he saw to his surprise, that he was very close to his destination. It was only a couple of streets away. He decided to leave the car where it was and walk the rest of the way.

Prince Valerie and Damion were returning home after doing some shopping for groceries. But as they strolled through Docklands Prince Valerie had his mind on another form of nourishment – every time an attractive woman passed by the

Prince would stare at her throat and salivate. 'I'm definitely going on the prowl tonight,' he told Damion. 'I'm absolutely starving.'

'Whatever you say, sire,' said Damion who, weighed down with all the shopping, wasn't in a good mood. Then he came to a sudden stop and exclaimed, 'Well, cut out my tongue and call me dumb. I don't bloody believe it!'

The Prince stopped too. 'What are you raving about?'

'Look! Look!' Damion cried excitedly, 'It's *him!*' He tried to raise an arm to point but the weight of the fully laden carrier bags prevented him, so he pointed with his nose.

The Prince looked up the street but couldn't see anything out of the ordinary. 'That hit on the head has really screwed you up,' he told his sorcerer.

'That man crossing the road by the traffic lights! It's Travis!'

The Prince peered ahead. He could see the man but he was too far away for him to recognize. 'Are you sure?'

'Yes, I'm positive! Come on, quick, before we lose him!'

Despite the weight of the carrier bags Damion started to run – well, stagger – down the street. The Prince shrugged and followed.

Travis hesitated at the entrance to the tall black glass and blue steel building that was Prenderghast's company headquarters. Then he squared his shoulders and marched inside.

There was a security desk situated between the two elevators in the foyer. The guard on duty asked him to sign the visitors' book. As he leaned forward to sign the book, the Colt .45 fell from his waistband and hit the floor with a loud bang.

'Oops,' said Travis, and bent down quickly. He scooped it up and tucked it back under his coat.

'Dropped my . . . my filofax,' he told the guard and gave an embarrassed laugh.

'What's it made of? Cast-iron?' asked the guard.

'Ha ha,' said Travis and quickly signed his name. The guard gave him a clip-on security pass but said nothing else.

Travis hurried into the waiting elevator.

As the elevator rose towards the top floor Travis examined his feelings. They were not feeling good. His heart was in his mouth, he had butterflies in his stomach and his churning bowels had turned to water. Oh, and his balls were trying to return to their pre-pubescent state.

The elevator came to a halt and the doors slid open to reveal Prenderghast's outer office. His secretary, sitting at her desk beside Prenderghast's inner door, frowned at him as he stepped into the office. 'You're two minutes late, Mr Thomson,' she told him sternly.

'Sorry, I got lost,' he mumbled sheepishly. Suddenly he was back at school again and on his way to see the headmaster. He hadn't really paid much attention to Prenderghast's secretary the last time he'd been there. She couldn't have been more than twenty-five but she sounded prim and imperious beyond her years. Yet she was very attractive, and, though she sat stiffly upright and wore a severe black dress, her body was excitingly voluptuous. He also noticed that her eyes were remarkably cat-like.

'Go in. Mr Prenderghast is waiting for you,' she informed him.

'Thanks,' he muttered. With his heart in his mouth etc etc, he opened the door and went into Prenderghast's office.

The Man himself, Gideon Leonard Prenderghast, was standing at the spectacular glass wall that was his window with his back to him. It seemed to Travis that Prenderghast had become even larger since he'd last seen him. He must have weighed at least twenty stone. His bulky figure cast a long shadow right across the office, which was odd as Travis knew that the sun was on the opposite side of the building.

Without turning around, Prenderghast said, in his deep, rumbling voice, 'Hello again, Travis. Please take a seat.'

Travis sat down in the chair placed in front of the desk. After several more moments of contemplating the London skyline, Prenderghast turned and sat down in his own chair, which was more like a throne than an office chair. He stared across the vast desk at Travis. Travis stared nervously back at him, taking in the round, ageless face, the slicked-back black hair and the dark, unfathomable eyes.

Travis cleared his throat. 'Errr, I'm sorry, Mr Prenderghast, but I had to do it. I had no choice. I couldn't let you distribute those VR helmets to kids . . .'

Prenderghast shrugged his huge shoulders. 'You have proved to be a serious nuisance to me, Travis,' he rumbled. 'And you have caused me much inconvenience by your actions.'

Travis tried to shrink himself down the crack at the back of the chair. 'Sorry,' he said in a very small voice. It was now or never. His hand began to move towards the Colt concealed under his jacket.

'But I can't blame you.'

Travis wasn't quite sure he'd heard right. 'Pardon?' he said. His hand stopped moving.

'I said I can't blame you. It was your ingenuity in using Princess Beatrice as a weapon that undermined me, but it was my fault that she is here in this world in the first place. I sent her and those two demons back with you from Samella in order to continue causing you irritation and to continue my amusement . . . and it backfired on me. I did not predict the affect she would have on people here . . .'

'You didn't?' said Travis, surprised. 'But I thought you were ominous . . . I mean . . .'

'Omnipotent?' said Prenderghast and gave a deep laugh, 'Hardly. Of course, by your world's pathetic standards I have powers beyond your puny imagination but I'm not omnipotent. And there rules that even I must obey. As a result . . .'

He was interrupted by a sudden commotion in the outer office. Travis turned. There were raised voices and then the door was flung open. Prince Valerie and Damion burst into the office, followed by the formidable secretary who looked extremely angry. Prince Valerie and Damion looked exultant. They both stared eagerly at Travis.

162

'At last! We've got you!' cried Prince Valerie. 'Revenge! Revenge!'

'Revenge!' echoed Damion. 'Heh, heh, heh, heh, heh . . .'

'I'm sorry, sir,' apologised Prenderghast's secretary. 'But they're . . .'

'I know,' said Prenderghast, raising a hand. 'So show them what you are.'

The secretary vanished and in her place was a large, black panther.

Until then Prince Valerie's and Damion's sole attention had been fixed on Travis. They hadn't even seemed to notice Prenderghast. But the sudden appearance of a snarling panther succeeded in drawing their attention away from Travis.

'What the. . . ?' said the Prince.

Damion looked at the panther and then at Prenderghast. Realization dawned. 'Uh oh,' he said.

'What is it?' asked the Prince, still in the dark.

Damion said, 'Sire, I think we have a problem . . .'

'Who's the big, fat bastard?' asked the Prince, pointing at Prenderghast.

'Sire, I think we should go,' said Damion. He grabbed the Prince by the sleeve and started to pull him back towards the door. But the snarling panther moved behind them, barring their way.

The Prince looked confused. 'Damion, what is going *on?*'

'Sire, he's One of Them . . .'

The gold sovereign finally dropped. 'Oh . . .' said the Prince. Then he gave Prenderghast an obsequious smile. 'Sorry for the intrusion, sir. A case of mistaken identity. We thought your friend here was someone we wanted to seriously mutilate. But, gosh, he isn't, so if you don't mind we'll be on our way . . .'

Prenderghast clicked his fingers. Prince Valerie and Damion instantly became frozen to the spot. They resembled a pair of waxwork dummies. The incongruous obsequious smile remained stuck on the Prince's face.

The panther disappeared and became the secretary again. She briefly bowed her head to Prenderghast and left. Somehow Travis knew that Prenderghast hadn't got her from an office temp agency.

'As I was saying before I was so rudely interrupted,' said Prenderghast. 'As a result of my stupidity it gives me no pleasure at all to inform you that I owe you one. In fact, according to the rules, more than one.' He gave a pained smile.

'You mean. . . ?'

'I'm afraid so.'

Travis sat up straight in his chair and grinned.

On the set of *Damned and Fancy* at Pinewood Studios, Travis felt as useful as a scriptwriter on a film set. The film crew were preparing to shoot the scene where Travis and company were about to escape from Prince Valerie's castle via the window in Princess Beatrice's sleeping chamber. The set didn't bear much resemblance to the reality, Travis had thought when he first saw it, if the word 'reality' could in any way be applied to Samella. The actual sleeping chamber had been quite small and Travis remembered how crowded it had been with all of them in it, but the set version of it was vast. You could stage Wagner's *The Ring* in it with room to spare.

The director, a hot young tyro who was already getting offers from Hollywood, was deep in discussion with the lighting cameraman, a grizzled industry veteran who could make an old shoe look great on the screen. With Beatrice he didn't even have to try. Travis had seen some of the rushes and Beatrice appeared incandescent. She was going to be the movie phenomenon of the century.

None of the cast were yet present on the set. Beatrice was no doubt in her huge, luxury trailer giving her hairdresser and make-up man a hard time. Travis rarely saw Beatrice much these days. She lived in an incredibly expensive flat in Mayfair, featured on more glossy magazine covers than Elizabeth Hurley, and moved in social circles far out of his range. He really only saw her on the set, and now and then she was gracious enough to acknowledge his existence.

Travis became aware of a haze of whiskey fumes. Harry Adam Knight had arrived. He stood beside Travis, swaying slightly. ''Lo, Travis,' he said. 'Seen the new rewrites?'

'Yes,' said Travis. 'And I'm not happy.' Jack had hired another script writer at the last minute, a young American kid who appeared to be still in the throes of puberty and was spattered with acne. 'More of my best lines have gone. And yours too.'

'I don't give a raw prawn, sport, and nor should you,' said Harry. 'You get used to that in this flaming business. You've got to leave your ego at home otherwise it'll get flushed down the dunny pan. The important thing is to get paid.'

'I suppose you're right,' muttered Travis, unconvinced.

A bald man in his mid-forties and dressed like a colour-blind American professional golfer went over to the director and the lighting cameraman and started haranguing them. Jack was back in his human form. As part of Travis's arrangement with Prenderghast, Jack was to regain his human body but he requested, and Prenderghast reluctantly agreed, that he could choose to be either whenever he wanted. This seemed an odd choice to Travis, but Jack had said, 'Look, there are advantages at times to being a small, flying demon. Besides, think of the movie. It would cost a fortune to replace me with a special effect!' And that's what had happened – whenever Jack the demon was needed for a scene, Jack the producer would rush off to answer an urgent phone call or something and Jack the demon would appear. So far no one had commented on the fact that the two of them were never together at the same time, to Travis's amazement. No wonder Superman got away with it for all those years. One thing Jack had done while in his human form was to fly back to LA and confront his wife, Candice, who had been less than happy to see that her husband was still alive. He had regained control of his company from her and – in his own words – '. . . fired

165

all those New Age fruits and aroma-friggin'-therapy assho-les!'

'Uh oh,' said Harry. 'Raving ratbag and galah alert on your port side.'

Travis looked and saw Prince Valerie and Damion heading towards him. They both had their scripts with them and they looked very annoyed. 'Travis, Harry . . . I want a word with you!' cried the Prince. 'And so do I!' said Damion.

Travis sighed. He knew what was coming.

'These rewrites on today's scenes!' said the Prince angrily, waving the multi-coloured screenplay in Travis's face. 'They're useless! You've cut out some of my best lines! What are you trying to do? Cut me out of the picture altogether?'

'Yeah, and the same goes for me,' said Damion. 'My part is getting smaller and smaller. I might as well've stayed in bed today!'

'For a start, Damion,' said Travis, 'you weren't originally even involved in this scene back in Samella. And secondly, as I keep telling you, neither Harry nor I are responsible now for any last-minute changes in the script. It's all the work of the Acne Kid. If you have any complaints take them up with Jack.'

This idea clearly didn't appeal to them. Travis had realized that they were now scared of Jack. Muttering and looking sulky they walked off.

'What a pair of mattress-munching drongos,' said Harry.

'They're a pain, I agree,' said Travis. 'But I prefer them like this than to the way they used to be.' As another part of his arrangement with Prenderghast they had been stripped of all their Samellian powers and attributes. Valerie was no longer a vampire and Damion was an ex-sorcerer. They were now ordinary human beings, if rather odd-looking ones. Stony broke and homeless – the owners of the Docklands penthouse had automatically come out of their spell in Guatemala and rushed back to England where they promptly evicted the squatters – they had gratefully accepted roles in the film playing themselves. They weren't too hot as actors –

though Valerie showed some potential – but at least they looked the part.

Prenderghast was gone. A week after their meeting in his office he disappeared while on a cruise on his yacht. His dead body was found in the sea some days later. But Travis wasn't fooled. He knew Prenderghast wasn't dead. It was just the way of making an exit from this particular time zone. He had a terrible suspicion that their paths would cross again, some day, somewhere.

Sharon arrived. Because Jack was aiming for a '15' certificate she wasn't naked for her part in the movie but was wearing a small, black leather bikini instead. She kissed Travis on the cheek and said, 'Where are we eating tonight?'

'Wherever you like, darling,' he told her.

'I fancy Chinese.'

'Then Chinese it will be.'

She kissed him again and then wandered over towards the director. She and Travis were now living together. As another part of his arrangement with Prenderghast she had been – with her agreement – 'de-fanged'. She was no longer a succubus but far from being an ordinary human being, and Travis could certainly testify to that.

'Bonzer little filly you have there, Travis,' said Harry, admiringly.

'I couldn't put it better myself,' said Travis.

'What are you two lazy bastards doing just hanging around?' It was Jack. Travis found him just as annoying when he was human as when he was a demon. But at least his breath smelt marginally better.

'We're hanging around, Jack,' Travis told him. 'We haven't got anything else to do, thanks to you.'

'Well, it's time you got back to work,' said Jack.

'You've sacked the Acne Kid?'

'I don't mean on this screenplay, I mean the sequel!'

'Sequel? What sequel?'

'The sequel you're going to start writing today!' He clapped his hands briskly. 'Now get cracking!' He strode off.

'Whacko-the-diddle-oh,' said Harry.
Good grief, thought Travis. *Here we go again.*

The BRITISH FANTASY SOCIETY

There is a group of people who know all the latest publishing news and gossip. They enjoy the very best in fiction from some of the hottest new talents around. They can read articles by and about their favourite authors and know in advance when those authors' books are being published. These people belong to the British Fantasy Society.

The BFS publishes a regular Newsletter as well as numerous magazines containing fantasy and horror fiction, speculative articles, artwork, reviews, interviews, comment and much more. They also organise the acclaimed annual FantasyCon convention to which publishers, editors and authors flock to hear the announcement of the coveted British Fantasy Awards, voted on by the members.

Membership of the British Fantasy Society is open to everyone. The annual UK subscription is £15.00 which covers the Newsletter and the magazines. To join, send monies payable to 'The British Fantasy Society', together with your name and address, to:

**THE BFS SECRETARY,
c/o 2 HARWOOD STREET,
STOCKPORT, SK4 1JJ**

Overseas membership:
£18 Europe, $32 USA and £23
everywhere else in the world.

The BFS reserves the right to raise membership fees.
Should the fee change, applicants for
membership will be advised.